SEARCH FOR THE CITY OF GOLD
RICK AND ROSE SINCLAIR ADVENTURE #3

RUSSELL JAMES

SEVEREDPRESS

SEARCH FOR THE CITY OF GOLD

Dedication

*For Christy,
my Rose on all my adventures*

CHAPTER ONE

Charleston, South Carolina, 1938

Rose Sinclair looked out from behind the curtains at the crowd on the Charleston auction house floor. The turnout was much better than she'd expected. Every seat was filled, and most by men in suits who had traveled from as far away as Maine. To the left of the stage, the auctioneer prepared himself behind a podium.

Rose was no stranger to selling antiques, but not on this large a scale. She and her husband Rick ran the Treasure Hunters Antiques shop in Savannah, but this collection of pirate-themed pieces was too large to bring back to their shop, and too valuable to risk moving very far. So they had opted for the auction in the same city as the collection.

Rose and Rick had become the custodians of this collection after their recent, expensive adventure searching for the lost treasure of Blackbeard the pirate. They hadn't brought any pirate plunder home, but surviving attacks by giant caimans and the spells of long-dead witches were pretty good consolation prizes. But if everything sold according to estimates, their commission managing this auction would make them whole again, with a little left over for their time and trouble.

Rick stepped up beside her. He flashed that movie-star smile of his. The auction idea had thrilled him from the beginning. He had a penchant for gambling, so an auction's uncertain outcome and potential huge upsides were right up his alley. Rose preferred small, well-considered acquisitions sold at reasonable rates to collectors. Rick relished the oddball purchase and its rare, bonanza resale. They clashed over their different approaches, but so far, the combination of the two had allowed their shop to survive the Great Depression.

Her husband's strong jaw and jet-black hair with a razor part on the side gave him a dashing look. He'd grown out a pencil moustache like Errol Flynn's after someone had mentioned their resemblance. His knowledge of antiques wasn't the best, but his broad shoulders and large biceps came in handy when they had to move some.

He handed her the final list of items to be auctioned. "All the paperwork is signed. At the end of this auction, we walk away with twenty-five percent of the gross."

"I'm surprised at the number and caliber of the bidders," Rose said.

"People will come out for a collection of genuine Blackbeard artifacts."

"But most of the stuff in the warehouse wasn't."

"Shh, not so loud."

Rose's eyes narrowed. "What did you do?"

"Me? I may have mentioned to one or two people, completely as a hypothetical, that items in the auction could have been taken from the wreck of his ship, the *Queen Anne's Revenge*, but could not be listed as such because of some murky salvage rights."

"That's not true."

"I never said it was," Rick said. "Now what the rumor mill churned my innocent statements into is completely out of my control."

"That's dishonest."

"The auction catalog doesn't claim anything is from the *Queen Anne's Revenge*, and that's what people should use to guide their bidding. If they don't, well, what can I do?" Rick made a dismissive wave with his hand. "And besides, all those stuffed shirts bidding out there are buying for rich people up North who are going to stick whatever it is in their smoking room and never look at it again. At the worst, this is a victimless crime, if it's even a crime at all."

Rose was pretty sure that a crime had been committed somewhere in Rick's little pre-auction performance. Now she just had to hope that no one caught wind of his scheme.

Two hours later, the auction was down to its last lot. Backstage, Rick had kept a running count of the total throughout the event. A flurry of bids crisscrossed the room and the gavel fell on the final item, a set of dueling pistols.

The auctioneer wished all the attendees a good night and the room began to empty.

Rick added the price to his list and summed up the total. "We're going to make a tidy sum here."

Rose looked at the number. It wasn't that large.

"This barely covers the expenses for the trip to Blackbeard's Island. You fronted a lot of money to your flyboy friend Humphrey to transport us down there. Subtract that, and there's not much left. But at least it won't have a minus sign in front of it. This cash will only keep us afloat for the next few months."

"Just long enough for me to bring in a few more of my unique, can't miss finds."

"You mean *can't sell* finds?" Rose said. "Just leave the purchasing to me, please."

Rose flipped through the final auction sale list and then looked at the catalog. "What happened to the sword?"

"What sword?"

Rose gritted her teeth. Rick's innocent act never sounded the remotest bit innocent. "Eighteenth century rapier, engraved hand guard, single ruby in the handle. *That* sword."

"Oh, glad you reminded me. Yeah, I made a great pre-sale swap for that."

"Swap? That sword was worth enough to buy us a new truck."

"As if we needed one," Rick said. "The point is, I traded up in value, as I always do."

"You'd trade a cow for magic beans if I didn't stop you."

"This time you'll be glad that you didn't. Come see."

Rick led her back to a deserted corner of the auction house. There, on a table, rested a blocky wood carving of a head at about twice life size. The style was Central American, probably Aztec from the face's broad features and the ring of glyphs that ran around the base.

"This," Rick said, like he was introducing royalty at a state dinner, "is from a consignment of artifacts brought back by an expedition deep into the jungles of Mexico. One-of-a-kind, thousands of years old. This will be worth way more than that old sword could be."

Rose picked up the head. It was much heavier than she'd expected. She examined several sides of it, then set it down and sighed.

"First, the glyphs on it are Aztec, so it could only be hundreds of years old," Rose said. "Second. this is a fake. Who did you get this from?"

"Fake? That's solid mahogany. I got it from a friend of mine who has an excellent reputation."

"You don't have any friends with excellent reputations. And this is made of pine with a mahogany stain."

"That can't be. That wood is strong as iron. Watch."

Rick took a knife from his pocket and flipped it open. He placed the blade against the side of the head and made a quick downward stroke. A giant shaving of wood curled up in front of the knife, exposing soft, yellow pine behind it.

Rick's jaw sagged. "I can't believe Lefty would cheat me."

"I can't believe someone named Lefty wouldn't."

Rose looked closer at the exposed pine. The grain did not match along the center of the gash, like it had been made from two separate pieces instead of carved from a single block. She took the knife from Rick's hand and wedged it into the seam in the middle. The two pieces were not glued together. She ran the knife blade further down the side and hit something hard. A quick scraping of the wood in that area uncovered a contemporary metal hinge.

"That confirms this carving's a fake," Rick sighed.

"It also shows that this head conceals something inside it," Rose said.

She ran the knife blade around the edge of the head, scratching the varnish and stain from a seam that went all the way around. There was no clue to find the clasp or lock that held it closed. She set the head back down.

"There has to be a way to open this."

"I have an axe at home," Rick offered.

"What? No! We can't risk damaging whatever is hidden inside by using too much force. It isn't a piggy bank."

Rick picked up the head and began to examine it from all angles. "I saw this detective movie once where there was a secret safe behind a painting. The release was hidden in the frame design."

Rick began to squeeze random features on the head.

"Rick, there's no way that—"

Rick pressed the right eye and the right ear at the same time. Something clicked in the carving and the front half of the head popped open.

"Voila," Rick said. "Hollywood to the rescue again,"

He opened the head. In a rectangular hollow in the middle lay a slab of glossy volcanic obsidian. Into it were carved a randomly arranged set of hieroglyphs, with arrows pointing from one glyph to another. Other symbols like a string of Vs and squiggly lines crossed the stone as well.

Rose gingerly removed the slab. It was a fraction of an inch thick and she was afraid it would shatter if she dropped it. No wonder someone had made the head as a decorative case for it.

Taking out the slab revealed a piece of paper hidden beneath it. Rick picked it up and held it alongside the slab. It contained a list of the hieroglyphs and an English translation beside each. The list included the words Tenochtitlan, Cholula, Cuahnahuac, and Tollocan. The last one on the list was Tezpaluca.

"I knew trading for this was a sure bet," Rick said. "I had a feeling that…whatever that black thing is, was inside waiting to be discovered."

"It's a map," Rose said. "And I recognize some of those names. They're Aztec cities."

Rick stared at her, waiting for more.

"The Aztec were the native people in Mexico when the Spanish arrived, but they had been there for two hundred years before that. They supposedly had a great empire, but many of the cities were lost to the jungle after the empire collapsed."

Rick's eyes lit up. "Didn't the Spanish go there in search of gold and jewels?"

"Especially looking for Tezpaluca. The city supposedly had been a great seat of Aztec power, possibly the source of the tales of a city with streets of gold."

"Well, if it's on a map, it must be more than mythical. And if the Spanish never found it, that can only be because Fate has decreed that you and I are supposed to."

Rose scoffed. "You think the two of us are going to slash our way through the jungle and find a lost city?"

"The two of us? Don't be ridiculous. We'll bring someone who can help with the locals."

"Don't you dare say Humphrey."

"Of course, Humphrey. He flies all over Central America, and he speaks Spanish. Plus, he can help with any heavy lifting. We'll give him a cut of what we find. We owe him for nearly getting him killed on Blackbeard's Island."

"It's going to take a lot of verification that this is authentic before I agree to this new wild goose chase."

"I'll start on that as soon as we get home."

"And this time we need an actual plan, not some seat-of-the-pants adventure."

Rick puffed his chest. "I excel at planning."

"No, you don't. This idea is terrible."

"This idea is spectacular. I've got an instinct for this kind of thing."

Rose sighed. What her husband had an instinct for was biting off a bit more than he could chew. She had a bad feeling this next expedition would be no different.

CHAPTER TWO

The day after Rose and Rick returned to Savannah, Rose began her research into Aztec culture. She started with the encyclopedia sets in the shop and some articles in old National Geographic magazines. That research gave her the basics.

The Aztec had ruled an empire in what was now Mexico for centuries before Hernando Cortez landed at present day Veracruz with several hundred fortune hunters. Montezuma II ruled the empire with an army of fierce warriors. But while the Aztecs were advanced in many technologies such as irrigation, stone construction, and farming, weapons were not on that list. A company of armored Spaniards with tempered steel swords and firearms brought the entire empire to its knees. Imported diseases such as smallpox did their parts and may have killed off half the population in a short time. By 1521, the Spanish controlled the capital and the empire crumbled. The mythical city of gold, Tezpaluca, was never found.

Rose now had a general picture, but she was going to need a lot more details before she agreed to head into the jungles of Mexico. It was time to call in a favor.

Two hours later she stood in front of the main library at Martyn University. The sandstone building hosted a bell tower that soared over the rest of the campus. Founded after the Civil War, it catered to the elite families in coastal Georgia and South Carolina. That meant it had a healthy endowment and benefactors ready to finance the university's purchase of historically important artifacts. The chair of the History department, Professor Bartholomew Keene, had purchased a number of such artifacts from Rose in the past, and always at a reasonable price.

The time had come to "call in her marker" as her husband would say.

Professor Keene hustled up the sidewalk as fast as his round belly and relatively short legs could carry him. He held

7

one hand to the top of his head to keep his sad little bowler hat in place.

"Sorry to keep you waiting!" His reedy voice barely made it out between his panting. "Students. Exams. Parents. The perfect storm this afternoon. Follow me."

The professor led her inside and past the ancient librarian manning the front desk. The frumpy woman raised her eyebrows at the sight of someone outside the academic hierarchy breaching the walls of her sanctum. But shielded by the authority of Professor Keene, Rose passed by unmolested.

The professor took her upstairs where books lined shelves that seemed to stretch on forever. He walked her to a locked door at the far end of the room. His keys jangled as he spun them in the lock. He eased open the door and waved her in.

Professor Keene turned on the lights to reveal shelves full of very old books. Cracked and frayed bindings stared out at her from tightly-packed rows. The room smelled as if the stale air had not turned over in centuries. Two wooden desks that looked like dorm room castoffs sat in the middle of the room.

"Ta da," the professor said. "You have entered Martyn University's holy of holies, the Research Room. Here we keep all the delicate and rare books in our collection, as well as the personal papers donated to the university."

"Personal papers?"

"Oh yes. We even have the papers of Benjamin Martyn, our namesake who was one of the Georgia colony's founders."

Rose wasn't about to admit she'd never heard of old Benjamin.

"What you want is down here," the professor continued.

He led her over to one corner and pointed to a shelf containing several handbound volumes that looked incredibly fragile.

"These are our Fernandina collection. By means I don't want to admit to, Georgians came into possession of these Spanish colonial documents from the town of Fernandina during the Patriot's War of 1812. If you're willing to apply yourself, somewhere in the trove are records of Spanish activity throughout the Americas. The records are, of course, in Spanish. But there are accompanying translations in the notebooks beside them. They were done by graduate students over thirty years ago, so they're a bit incomplete."

Rose reached into her bag and pulled out a pair of cotton gloves. "I'm ready to work with what you have."

"Splendid. I will leave you to your own devices. The library closes at five. Miss Millar at the front desk is overly protective, so I will assure her that you don't need to be searched for pilfered books as you depart."

"Thank you, Professor."

"Not at all. You'll keep me first to be notified if you come across any Colonial artifacts in your acquisitions, I trust?"

"As always, you get first call."

The professor left her alone and shut the door behind him. She went to the table and set down her bag. From the bag she pulled out two pieces of paper. Each contained pencil tracings from the Aztec head. One was of the map on the inside, and one was of the hieroglyphs around the neck of the head. At the top of the map page, she'd written *Tezpaluca* in big block letters.

She put on her gloves. There wouldn't be time to read everything in the collection. She was going to page through books that seemed relevant and hope to find this city's name somewhere. She'd see just how close the Spanish came to finding the City of Gold.

CHAPTER THREE

Rick couldn't find Humphrey.

A former military ace in Sopwith Camels during the Great War, Humphrey Custis was now a civilian pilot flying his own weathered-looking Ford Tri-motor. He scraped by making a living with a combination of cargo hauls, passenger flights, and middle-of-the-night missions of dubious legality. The closed military airfield Humphrey flew out of had been gifted to the county after the war, and the locals had promptly let it go to seed. But there were no parking or landing fees, which was just the right price for Humphrey, not to mention that there were no prying eyes watching his comings and goings.

Rick hadn't seen Humphrey in or around his plane, though Humphrey's car was parked nearby. The closed control tower was the only building on the site, so Rick figured his pal must be in there, escaping the hot Georgia sun.

Like everything else at the airfield, including Humphrey, the control tower had seen better days. The roof was missing shingles and patches of peeling paint made the walls look like they had a fungal disease. The windows on the ground level were too dirty to see through. Rust marred the old metal door that stood slightly ajar.

Rick pushed it open and the hinges squealed in protest.

The small room stank like a gym locker room. Rick couldn't make out all the details in the fuzzy light, and that was probably a good thing. Drying clothes hung from a line strung across the room. On one side, a dresser missing all its drawers had assumed duty as a half-assed pantry and housed a collection of canned goods and some plates. A military cot hugged the other wall. Humphrey lay on it above the blanket. Rick counted himself lucky the man was fully clothed.

"Humphrey!" he shouted.

Humphrey woke up with a start and jumped to his feet. "Rick! I must have done nodded off there."

"Are you living in here?"

"As far as anyone knows, no." Humphrey ushered him out of the building and slammed the door shut behind him. "Had a bit of a misunderstanding, you might say, with my landlord."

"Meaning he understood that you were supposed to pay your rent?"

"I explained how I simply owed it to him. I wasn't cheating him out of it." Humphrey's Southern drawl was slow and thick. "Damned if he didn't toss me out anyhow."

"I thought you had a cargo run to the Bahamas last week?"

"That client, he had himself an untimely run-in with the FBI. Damn income taxes are outright un-American."

"This is your lucky day," Rick reached in and handed Humphrey a wad of cash. "We sold those pirate artifacts and this should cover your expenses for that trip."

Relief crossed Humphrey's face. "I tell you what, that's a lifesaver right there. Some of that food in there's got some bulges to the cans."

"Now if you want," Rick said, "I can double that for you. I've got a tip on the sixth race tomorrow. This horse can't lose."

Humphrey stuffed the cash into his pocket. "Nothing doing. Bird in the hand and all that."

"Your loss. Aside from that, I have the opportunity of a lifetime for you."

Humphrey took a step back. "Oh, no. Your last 'opportunity' to get rich almost got me killed."

"This time's going to be totally different. No giant monsters, just a quick hop down to Mexico. A couple of days, at the most, and then right back here."

"Back here carrying what?"

"Gold, dear Humphrey. As much as your tired little plane can hold. All there for the taking."

A look of curiosity crossed Humphrey's face. "How's about you show me where."

Humphrey led Rick over to the Tri-motor. He entered through the cabin door, and returned in a moment with a very battered map of Mexico.

"Looks like you've been to Mexico a few times," Rick said.

"Not according to my official flight log. Now where we going?"

Rose had shown Rick in general where the map indicated Tezpaluca was. He made a vague circular motion with his finger over the southeast part of Mexico. "Right about here."

Humphrey squinted at the map. "There's a whole lot of nothing right about there."

"We have a map. Sort of. Working on the details."

"Well, we can take ourselves a boat ride up this river here," Humphrey said. "If ya'll want to make a vacation out of it. But I think a floatplane's gonna be our best bet. We can land anywhere on the river."

"And you can borrow a float plane?"

"Well, I can rent one. But that's gonna mean some upfront cash."

"What a coincidence," Rick said. "I just handed you cash."

"This expense ain't coming out of *my* pocket."

"This isn't an expense. It's a loan to yourself. The gold we find will repay it right away, with interest. Just don't get greedy and overload the plane. We can make two trips."

Humphrey looked wary. "Rose is coming with us?"

"Of course."

"She likes a case of the chiggers more than being in the same room as me."

"What?" Rick feigned shock. "She likes you fine."

"There's times you can sell a good lie," Humphrey said. "This ain't one of them."

"Look, this is going to be easy as pie," Rick said. "You fly us in. We find gold. You fly us out. You just find us a plane that can walk on water."

CHAPTER FOUR

Rick returned to the shop to find Rose in the work area behind the public portion of the store. She sat at her workbench, red hair tied back in a ponytail, blue eyes intently studying pages of notes. An atlas opened to Mexico lay on the bench beside her.

He walked up and draped an arm around her shoulders. "Rosie, hard at work on the research, I see."

"The university had a Spanish-era treasure trove, just as I'd heard," she said. "I'll bet there is even more information at some of the Atlanta universities."

"No dice. We need to keep knowledge of this little trip within a tight, trustworthy group."

"That from the man who just recruited Humphrey. I assume he agreed to be part of this scheme?"

"Scheme?" Rick said. "More like *amazing plan*. He was thrilled the moment I mentioned it. Even offered to front the money for some of the expenses."

Rose gave him a sideways look. "He offered or you goaded him into that decision?"

"That detail isn't as important as the result, that he's onboard. Now, what did you find out at the university?"

Rose rearranged some of the pages in front of her. "There was Spanish documentation of the city of Tezpaluca, or of the tales told about that city. It was one of a dozen in the empire, all of differing sizes. This one particularly caught Cortez's attention because of the City of Gold rumors about it, many corroborated by natives who claimed they or relatives saw it."

Rose picked up one page. "The people worshipped the god of the night sky, Tezcatlipoca. And from what others reported, that worship was so complete that the entire population slept all day and functioned only after sunset."

"A whole city on the night shift?"

"So they said. It was also recorded that because of that, the people could see in the dark, even lost the pigments that colored their skin."

"That sounds like nonsense."

"It may be that the locals started to give them the same attributes they'd seen in cave-dwelling creatures. At any rate, the other cities gave this one a wide berth. And Aztec kKing Montezuma II even left them alone as long as their tribute was paid. Tezpaluca paid once per year, instead of monthly like the other cities. The payment was made by a company of warriors in long, feathered, hooded cloaks that covered them head to toe. This annual tribute probably seemed much greater than the other cities' monthly tribute gave. Maybe that's how Tezpaluca got the reputation for being a city of riches."

"Or it really was rich and sounds like my kind of place," Rick said. "So where is it?"

"The obsidian map we have places the city at the headwaters of the Usmacinta River, which would have been the far reaches of the Aztec Empire."

"Excellent! Humphrey's going to get us a floatplane so we can land right on the river instead of spending forever on a boat fighting an upriver current."

"And not taking gold on a boat back downriver makes keeping our find secret a lot easier," Rose said.

"Two positive results from just one of my fantastic decisions."

Rose rolled her eyes at his self-congratulations. "Some of the stories I read were unnerving. The Aztecs were brutal. Ritual human sacrifice and sports that ended in death for the loser were commonplace. Tezpaluca was no different, and maybe worse than the rest. Drinking human blood was central to their culture."

"Not much to be worried about since everyone who was there is long dead." Rick had a thought. "Wait a minute. If everyone there was asleep all day, what kept Montezuma from marching an army in at noon and killing everyone in their sleep?"

"The city was reported to be defended by creatures, all enhanced by the power of Tezcatlipoca, ready to slaughter invaders in the daylight, and no one dared enter the city after nightfall. Spirits that snatched and devoured intruders were said to haunt the jungle."

"That's a little farfetched."

"But the stories were no doubt inspired by dangerous wildlife, which might still inhabit the area."

"That was hundreds of years ago," Rick said. "We're a little better at defending ourselves in 1938 and, just like there's no mountain lions in Georgia anymore, I'm sure local game hunters have eradicated most dangerous predators down there. But don't worry. I'll be my usual careful self."

"That's what I'm afraid of." Rose gave Rick a deadly serious look. "We should rethink this idea. At one point, Cortez had sent several companies on missions to take this city. Only one survivor from the third mission made it back. After that, not only did Cortez stop trying, he had the location of Tezpaluca wiped from all the Spanish maps. Think how bad it would have to be for treasure hunters to give up trying to conquer a city with streets of gold."

Rick dismissed her concern with a wave of his hand. "These are four-hundred-year-old ghost stories. These people thought sea monsters lived at the edge of the map of a flat Earth. The first thing they did when anything bad happened was blame the supernatural."

"You think all this evidence is nonsense?"

"No, the opposite. All this evidence proves that the City of Gold existed, that we have a map to get to it, and that it was never cleaned out by the Spanish. Your research doesn't warn me off from going to find it, it encourages me. If it's half as rich as the Spanish said, we're going to come home wealthy and famous."

"If it's half as dangerous as the Spanish said," Rose replied, "we'll be lucky to come home at all."

CHAPTER FIVE

Three days later

Rose, Rick, and Humphrey were in Humphrey's plane headed for the city of Cortez on the southwestern side of Cuba. She'd read that the city was a hotbed of criminal activity. Rose knew Humphrey moved in places like that with ease, and feared her husband could do the same.

The flight had been uneventful, which amazed Rose given how tired Humphrey's Tri-motor looked and that the copilot was her barely-trained husband. Still, it wasn't until the wheels touched the Cuban airfield that she released her death grip on the armrests of her seat.

They taxied Humphrey's plane to an apron along the runway where, not a simple float plane awaited them, but a much larger flying boat. The three of them left Humphrey's plane and approached the flying boat.

The sight of it made Rose shudder. Humphrey's Tri-motor might have seemed a marginally sound aircraft, but at least it was a monoplane made of metal. Neither attribute applied to the contraption they were transferring to. The decades-old biplane had wings a hundred feet across and a boat-like body about half that long. Some very untrustworthy-looking cables ran between the wooden struts on the canvas wings. The body of the plane looked like an overstuffed cigar. Circular windows along the body promised an enclosed cabin for passengers, but the pilots flew from an open center cockpit between the top-wing-mounted twin engines. Black oil stains streaked the engine cowlings.

"What the hell is that thing?" Rose said.

"Why that there's an Aeromarine 75," Humphrey said. "The Navy and the Post Office used 'em all the time."

"Sure, twenty years ago." Rose squinted at the wing. "Is that plane covered in canvas?"

"Well, the wings are, but that hull there's been upgraded to solid veneer."

"So's my china cabinet," Rose said, "but I wouldn't fly somewhere in it."

A stout man in stained coveralls popped out of a hatch on the nose of the plane, climbed down a tiny ladder, and approached them. He had a shock of black wavy hair, a wrench in one hand, and a smudge of grease on his left cheek. The fact that the man was actively fixing something did not inspire Rose's confidence.

"Carlos!" Humphrey met the man and pumped his hand like he was getting water from a well. "*Buenos muchachos, amigo!*"

Carlos rolled his eyes. Rose didn't speak much Spanish, but even she knew what she just heard wasn't right. She punched Rick in the arm. "I thought you said Humphrey spoke Spanish."

"He knows all the important Spanish."

"Is everything ready?" Humphrey said to Carlos.

"Packed, fueled up, ready for takeoff. My bag is already on board."

Rose stepped forward to the two men. "Carlos is coming with us?"

"Got us one hell of a deal," Humphrey said. "This here plane comes with a full tank of gas and a pilot."

Rose thought it was bad enough having sketchy Humphrey in on this trip. There was no telling how much sketchier Humphrey's contacts would be. "That wasn't what we planned."

"We're landing a big plane on a narrow river," Rick said. "Would you rather Humphrey and I do it, or someone with a lot more hours in the plane?"

She had to admit that an experienced pilot would be a plus, especially in a creaky crate like this plane. "Was this old thing built during the war?"

"Sure enough," Humphrey said, "just like every other plane I flew back then. If it was good enough to help bring the Germans to their knees, it can sure get you to Mexico and back on one tank of gas. Plus, it can carry two thousand pounds of cargo, even something dense like gold."

"It's perfect, Rose," Rick said.

"It's ancient."

"I prefer time-tested," Humphrey said. "And Carlos and I, we've flown this very plane into Mexico before."

"Doing what?" Rose said.

"The kind of discreet cargo runs I specialize in."

"Just great."

Two more men approached the plane chatting in Spanish. Each carried a pack. Both were beefy, sunburned, and scarred. They made Savannah dockworkers look like Boy Scouts. Both gave Rick and Rose a sideways look and then climbed on board.

"And who are they?" Rose said. "Stewardesses?"

"All part of the deal," Humphrey said. "Two of Carlos' men, Manuel and Geraldo, are coming along to help us. We may need to do some jungle chopping to uncover the lost city."

"And we'll definitely have to do some heavy lifting hauling all the gold we find out of the jungle," Rick said.

"You knew about all these details before we left, didn't you?" Rose said.

"Rosie, I didn't agree to anything that wasn't in your best interest."

"This is so typical of your plans," Rose seethed. "I always get surprises along the way, and none of them are good."

"C'mon, Rosie. Would you really rather be traipsing through the jungle alone, or surrounded by all these personal bodyguards?"

"The way those men look," Rose said, "I'm wondering who would guard me from the guards."

***

The plane had forward and rear cabins. Between them was a mechanical room containing the plane's fuel tanks and electrical system. Rick and Rose took seats in the forward cabin while Carlos' men and all the gear took the rear. Rick had a window seat for the flight into Mexico. Part of him missed having a windshield seat in the cockpit, but the other part of him was certain trying to pilot the flying boat would have exceeded his minimal skill set. He also didn't relish the idea of sitting up there exposed to the elements with an aircraft engine roaring in each ear.

The wicker cabin seats would have looked more at home on the front porch of a plantation home and their faded cushions had given up delivering comfort at least a decade ago. Rick had watched Rose shift and squirm in her seat the entire trip, just as uncomfortable as he was. He had no idea that this leg of their trip would be so grueling. He'd make it up to her. When they came home from this trip rich, he'd buy her a couch so comfortable she'd think she was floating on a cloud.

The Caribbean Sea had more shades of green and blue than Rick had ever seen in the murky Atlantic near Savannah. As the plane closed on the Mexican coast, Rick could see the bottom, even though the water still had to be fifty feet deep. The plane crossed a narrow, white beach and then the land surrendered to jungle. If there were any roads or villages down there, he couldn't see them. There must have been a lot of gold for the taking if conquistadors had hacked their way through all of that. Rick smiled at that heartening thought.

The plane crossed a muddy-looking river and banked to the left, following the river upstream. This had to be the Usmacinta River they'd seen on the map. He looked over at Rose sitting beside him. Her eyes were closed.

He nudged her. "Are you asleep?"

"No, I'm praying for divine intervention that we get safely back on the ground."

"We're over the river, so we're almost there."

Rose sighed. "That's the best news I've heard all day."

The engines cut back and the plane slowed. As it descended, Rick couldn't see the river anymore, and had to trust that Humphrey and Carlos had them lined up right on top of it. In a minute, they were at tree-top level. The engines roared once, then cut back to idle.

The plane dropped and hit the river like a boat dropped off the end of a pier. The hull slammed the water with a thud, and the entire plane shuddered. The hull skipped once, then settled into plowing the river with the grace of a garbage scow. The plane taxied a short distance, then the engines cut off. Chains rattled as an anchor dropped from the bow.

"See," Rick said. "Safe and sound on the ground."

"You mean on the water," Rose said, "and this old crate might start sinking at any moment."

Humphrey came back to the passenger cabin. "Welcome to Mexico!"

Rose jumped up from her chair, as if more willing to face the jungle than spend another second on the aircraft.

Humphrey opened the door on the side of the plane. Humid air redolent of the peaty smell of a jungle and the miasma of stagnant water rolled in from outside. The aircraft floated a dozen yards from the shore in murky water.

"Funny thing," Humphrey said. "Them Aztecs didn't leave us no dock."

He dragged an inflatable raft over to the door, pushed it out, and pulled a handle on the side. The raft inflated.

"Mind if I do the paddling?" Rick said to Rose.

"I insist," she said.

Carlos entered from the rear cabin with his two men in tow. He had a concerned look on his face. "I just inspected the bilge. We sprung a leak." He gave Humphrey a sharp look. "Probably the hard landing on the river."

Humphrey feigned offense. "Why, that landing was smoother than a piglet's belly."

Rose slapped Rick's shoulder. "I told you this plane would sink."

"No," Carlos said. "A hand pump will keep up with the leak. I'll have to stay here pumping."

"Someone should stay anyway," Rick said. "The last thing we need is to return laden with gold and find that the plane had slipped its anchor, or worse, been stolen by some passing locals. If there are any passing locals, that is."

"I'll stay," Humphrey volunteered, "and I'll patch the leak, even though it ain't my fault."

Rose gave Carlos and his two men a wary look. Rick could tell she was worried that with Humphrey at the plane instead of Carlos, the visiting team would outnumber Team Sinclair by three-to-two.

"It's okay," Rick whispered to her. "Better that Carlos be in charge of his men, no English translating and all that, right?"

Rose muttered a barely audible dissent, but ended up nodding.

Carlos looked hard at Humphrey. "If I come back to a sunken airplane, the best thing for you would be to be inside it."

"Why, she'll be good as new. Probably better. Ain't no plane I can't fix."

Rick didn't want to mention that this repair job would be more like working on a boat.

***

It took several trips to get the five of them and their equipment ashore. Manuel and Geraldo loaded up with the bulk of the gear. Rick and Carlos shouldered two heavy packs. Rose picked up a third, nearly-empty backpack. She sighed with frustration.

"I'm going to kick you both in the shins if you try treating me like a helpless female." She threw the pack at their feet. "Fill that up."

Rick had to smile. There was a reason he'd married this girl. He dropped his pack and took some pans out of it. "You sure now?"

"Just pack it."

Rick slid the cast iron pans into her pack and handed it back to her. She smiled and heaved it up on one shoulder. The added weight threw her off balance. Her eyes went wide and she stumbled sideways until she righted herself. She slipped the other shoulder strap into place.

"Happy now?" Rick said.

"Ecstatic. Let's get moving."

Carlos unfolded the map they'd marked with the probable city location. Then he took out a compass and shot an azimuth. "Ought to be this way. Not too far, either."

"It shouldn't be," Rose said. "They would have built the city as close as possible to the river, but out of the floodplain around it."

The group tromped through the jungle. The four men carried machetes, but the flora was not as dense as Rick had feared, so they kept them sheathed. The overhead canopy blocked a lot of light from reaching the ground, so most of the growth was small enough to walk around or over. Every few minutes Rick would glance over his shoulder to check on Rose and her burdensome backpack. She was keeping up, though with sweat on her brow and gritted teeth. It was a sure bet that she'd drop dead before admitting that the pack was too much for her.

Up ahead, a dark, furry shape lay on the ground. A breeze blew the branches overhead and it lay in a flickering patch of sunlight.

"Hold up," Rick said. "Whatever that is, I don't like the look of it."

Rick pulled his machete from his belt and pointed it at the form. He made a slow advance and didn't lower the blade until he was right on top of the shadowy shape.

A dead black jaguar lay on the ground. This close, it was possible to differentiate the black spots against the different shade of the black background. This animal was bigger than any jaguar he'd seen, even bigger than a lion.

The cause of its death was clear to see. A steel wire snare trap had caught one paw and the end was wrapped around a big tree. Even this large a cat couldn't break that free.

Rick waved the others forward.

When he stood next to the cat, Carlos gasped. "That's one big kitty."

"Jaguars are common here," Rose said. "But black ones are rare."

"You're a jaguar expert now?" Rick said.

"After I finished my Aztec research, I looked into local animals that might kill us. You know, just in case you got us into a situation like this."

"Now we know we need to keep an eye out for jaguars," Carlos said.

"We know something even more important," Rick said. "That snare means someone else is out here."

"You're right about that," said a voice behind them.

CHAPTER SIX

Rick spun around with his machete drawn. Carlos brandished his as well.

An older man with long, gray hair and round glasses stood a few feet away. He wore shorts, sandals and a tattered khaki button-down shirt. He raised his hands in surrender.

"Easy does it, now," he said. "I'm no more dangerous than that deceased jaguar."

"In my experience," Carlos said, "only dangerous people sneak up on someone."

"I've been studying in the field for over a month and learned to tread quite lightly." The man's distinct British accent was quite out of place in a Mexican jungle. "I'm Professor Clarence Dartmouth. My only threat to your safety would be boring you to death, but since we aren't in a lecture hall, that means you're quite safe."

Rose reached over and lowered Rick's machete to point at the ground. "We're Rose and Rick Sinclair. This is our pilot, Carlos, and his men Manuel and Geraldo."

Carlos touched the bill of his battered cap. "Pleasure to meet you."

"What brings you out here, Professor?" Rick said.

Clarence pointed to the jaguar. "Trying to catch a specimen of one of those."

Clarence went to the jaguar and knelt by its head. He loosened the snare from the cat's paw and set it aside. The snare didn't seem to have wounded the cat.

"Big cats are my specialty." Clarence pronounced specialty *spesh-i-a-li-tee*. "Genus *Panthera*, you know. Lions, tigers, why I've been known to stray into cheetahs. Heard stories of these rare, local jaguars and thought I'd have a go at trapping one. But I'll admit that snare was set for other game. I was gobsmacked to see a jaguar trapped by it."

Rick stifled a laugh at the professor's *jag-u-ar* pronunciation.

23

"I've read that black jaguars are rare," Rose said.

"Ah, yes, but these may be even more unique. The attributes of these local cats may qualify them as a distinct species. First is the size." Clarence raised the dead cat's paw and rotated the leg around the shoulder. "This creature is enormous for a jaguar, for any cat, actually. And it's much more muscular, more powerful than it would need to be to hunt the small prey here in the jungle."

"Maybe it overeats," Carlos said.

"No, dear boy, Nature doesn't work that way. She has every animal adapt to perfection to its niche in the environment. Being this big would mean it needed more prey than the jungle could provide, and it would be more difficult to hunt when the vegetation became dense. That was the first mystery of what I'm calling the greater jaguar."

"And the second mystery?" Rose said.

"Ah, an even greater one."

The professor wrenched open the mouth of the jaguar. Dead or not, watching the big cat reveal its jaws full of sharp teeth made Rick very uneasy. Then Clarence made it worse as he wrapped one of his fingers around the jaguar's long canine tooth.

"Now then, this tooth here is large, but even taking into account the larger animal, it is out of proportion to the other teeth. It is wider and much longer than a normal jaguar would have. Not to the extent seen in a *Smilodon*, of course, but still well outside the range of what we should see."

The professor yanked the cat's head so the palate pointed up. "And the most curious attribute is here. Look closely at the tip and you'll see a hole."

The three of them bent down for a closer look. Indeed, Rick saw a small hole at the tip.

"A cat with a cavity?" Rick said.

"No, a cat with venom. The structure resembles that of poisonous snakes. This confirms that the one skull I've been able to examine wasn't some kind of aberration."

"That's novel," Rose said.

"It's worse than that," Clarence corrected. "It's quite useless. Jaguars ambush hunt and are able to kill their prey with a single bite to the neck, then they tear them apart to eat.

There is no need for a jaguar to paralyze prey, because the prey dies almost instantly. That's especially true of this species which is much stronger than a common jaguar."

Rick thought this biology lesson was interesting, but he had some more pressing questions he needed answered. "So how did you get all the way out here in the middle of nowhere?"

"Canoe from the coast. My son and I paddled up here and set up a camp near where the greater jaguar were said to roam. Not too hard to find, really. Just asked the local people where they considered off-limits."

"So you're living in a village out here?" Rose said.

"There's not a village for a hundred miles. We've been tenting it out here."

"How do you stay supplied?" Rick said.

"Living off the land, so to speak. Fish from the river, wild plants, drinking rain water. It won't be mistaken for fine cuisine, but we get by."

Rose knelt down beside the professor. She examined the paw.

"I've seen snare traps at work. They leave some awful wounds, but this jaguar isn't scratched."

Clarence ran a hand through his hair. "Yes, that is a conundrum. As is the fact that it is dead and not alive. There aren't any signs of injury. I'd expect it to be standing here snarling at us right now."

Rick was beginning to be frustrated by this conversational sidetracking. They did have a treasure city to find. "So, Clarence, if there aren't any villages around here, how about any ancient ruins?"

"Haven't seen any, but we haven't traveled all that widely. Were you looking for an Aztec city, by chance?"

Rick's eyes narrowed. "Why would you ask that?"

"One of the native legends was that the jaguars were the embodiment of the souls of Aztec warriors killed defending a great city from the Spanish. The main problem with the myth is there's no city to back it up. And what else would you fine Americans be doing out here other than that?"

"Could be just trying to get away from it all," Rick said.

"Well, you've accomplished that. I'll let you go about your business, whatever that is. I need to push off for camp and get my son to help bring back this specimen. Its dissection should be quite illuminating."

"Why don't we help you bring it back," Rick offered, "and in exchange we sleep in your camp tonight. We'll start tomorrow fresh and you can be sure nothing scavenges this jaguar before you get to take a look at it."

"I say, splendid idea. With a few stout sticks we can make a jaguar litter."

"We'll help you find them," Carlos said.

He issued some orders in Spanish and then he and his two men began to root around the jungle for suitable fallen branches. Rose turned to Rick.

"What are you doing?" Rose whispered. "I thought you hated trusting strangers."

"This guy couldn't be more harmless. He seems on the level. We'll check out his story, and have a guaranteed safe place to sleep tonight. Then tomorrow, we find the lost City of Gold."

"You think it will be that easy?"

"Absolutely. There's nothing between us and those riches but a lot of ferns and palm trees."

"We didn't know there were giant jaguars prowling around until a few minutes ago," Rose said. "I have a bad feeling that won't be our last surprise out here."

CHAPTER SEVEN

After a short search, Carlos and his men returned with a pair of relatively straight branches eight feet long. The group soon had them under the jaguar's belly. Rick pitched in and with one person at the end of each pole, they lifted the jaguar. The cat lay on the sticks with all four paws dangling from the sides. The setup was surprisingly workable. But even with the weight divided by four, keeping the jaguar off the ground was a workout, especially with packs still on their backs.

Clarence led the way with Rose behind him. Soon they arrived at Clarence's camp, which was little more than two canvas tents facing a firepit between them. Clarence's son, a chubby man in his thirties with sandy hair, stood by the firepit. As he spied the group, he ducked into one tent, and reemerged with a hunting rifle.

"We're literally being welcomed with open arms," Rick said to Rose.

"It's quite all right, Edgar," Clarence called out. "The jaguar is dead and the people are friendly."

Edgar seemed to mull over whether his father was only saying that under duress, then decided he wasn't. He set down the rifle and went to a long table filled with books and papers behind the firepit. He cleared it to make room for the cat. The group set the jaguar down on the table.

Rick shook Edgar's hand. "I'm Rick Sinclair. That's Carlos, Manuel, and Geraldo, and this is my wife, Rose."

Edgar looked Rose over with an appraising eye. Rick chalked his poor manners up to being in the jungle alone too long and refrained from punching him. Rose, however, seemed about to exhibit less self-control. She liked being objectified about as much as she liked getting poison ivy.

"This jaguar has to weigh at least three hundred pounds," Clarence said.

His father's observation redirected Edgar's attention before Rick had to restrain Rose. Edgar turned back to the cat.

"Where did this specimen come from?" Edgar said.

"Caught in one of our snares."

Clarence took out a notebook and opened it to a page filled with very detailed pencil drawings of jaguars. He began to compare the dead cat to the pictures he'd penned.

Edgar glanced at the cat's uninjured feet. "It must have died of old age, because the snare wouldn't kill it."

"Quite a compelling mystery," Clarence said. "Which is why I want to start the dissection while I still have daylight to work with."

"I'd expect nothing less." Edgar's voice dripped with resignation.

"Our visitors will be spending the night," Clarence said. "Why don't you get them settled and start dinner for everyone?"

Edgar grumbled a response and turned toward the camp.

"For someone isolated in the jungle for a while," Rose whispered to Rick, "you'd think Edgar would be more excited to have company."

"Maybe hating company was why he decided to be isolated out in the jungle," Rick said.

Edgar led them to the firepit between the tents. Based on the contents of each tent, it looked like he and his father shared one, with the other used for their research.

"Set up wherever you like," he said.

"My men and I will just sleep under the canopy," Carlos said.

"It gets a bit buggy at night," Edgar said.

"Cuba has jungles. We are used to it."

Rick recruited Carlos to pick out a spot nearby to set up a tent for Rose and himself. As they erected it, Rick took the opportunity to get a better feel for Carlos. "You grew up in a place like this?"

"Pretty close," Carlos said. "Up in the mountains in Cuba. Poor as hell in a backwater village. I think my first words were 'I'm getting out of here.'"

Rick gestured to the jungle around them. "Mission accomplished. How did you end up flying your own plane?"

"At age 13 I ran off to Havana. I started out unloading planes at the airport, turned to helping fix them, then graduated to flying them. Lots of cargo coming in and out of Cuba."

Lots of illegal cargo, Rick thought.

"I bought this plane with my cut of a year's worth of runs. Lots of blood and sweat, you know? So Humphrey better take care of her."

"Humphrey has a lot of faults, but he treats aircraft like family. He'll care for yours."

"He'd better."

Soon the new addition to the camp had been erected. Carlos returned to his men and Rick and Rose moved their packs inside their tent. Outside by the firepit, Carlos and his men carried on a conversation in Spanish accentuated with some sly grins.

Rose dropped their tent flaps. "I'm only getting bits and pieces of the conversation Carlos and his men are having," Rose said, "but the tone of it is conspiratorial."

"I think you're reading more into it than is there. I talked with him and he seems legit. Plus, Humphrey vouches for them."

"So, wait. You trust the admitted smugglers and two strangers you just met in a Mexican jungle?"

"Well when you say it that way, it makes me sound foolish."

"Your words," Rose said, "not mine."

"Okay, how about we just keep one eye on Carlos and one eye on the professor?"

"And hope everyone else is keeping an eye out for jaguars," Rose said.

***

More out of a fear of inadvertent poisoning than any longing to exercise domesticity, Rose pitched in to help prepare dinner. It became a pot luck from the two groups. Edgar provided wild bananas and a root crop Rose didn't recognize and Carlos offered up some tinned beef. They all settled in around the firepit and began to eat off simple metal plates. Clarence completed his big cat autopsy in time to join them.

"This beef is bloody wonderful," Edgar said with his mouth full.

Rose speared what looked like an artery out of a chunk of meat and flicked it into the jungle. "You're joking, right?"

"Not in the least. I've had enough river fish and peccary to last a lifetime."

"What did you find out about the cat?" Rick asked Clarence.

Clarence paused eating. "Quite a bit. I believe that I solved the conundrum of the canine teeth. Just above the soft palete, the cat does have a venom gland. Like the local fer-de-lance snake, it seems this cat has developed the ability to deliver a toxin to its victims."

"As if being a giant cat isn't scary enough," Carlos said, "it shoots venom on top of that."

"Injects, actually," Clarence said. "This is really quite a discovery, well worth the tribulations of spending time in the jungle."

Rose didn't think Edgar seemed to share his father's enthusiasm. He just focused on the food on his plate.

"And I dare say I discovered a new mystery as soon as I solved the old," Clarence said. "As suspected, the cause of death was not the snare. It was dehydration."

"The poor thing had no access to water," Rose said.

"We set that snare yesterday. The jaguar wasn't trapped long enough to get to such an extreme level of dehydration. This creature was close to being internally mummified. Even its eyeballs had desiccated."

"What might cause that?" Rick said.

"Nothing plausible," Clarence said with a smile. "That makes it an even more splendid mystery."

"Speaking of mysteries," Edgar said, "what are you chaps doing mucking about out here anyway?"

"Searching for a lost Aztec city called Tezpaluca," Rick said.

Clarence laughed. "Well, we can't help you there. We haven't seen any hint of civilization, past or present, since we got here."

"When we head out tomorrow, why don't you come with us?" Rick said. "You can help us through the area you know, then maybe you'll learn more about the jaguars when we get to the places you don't."

Rose recoiled. This invitation was a bad idea. "Rick, I'm sure that Clarence wouldn't want to—"

"It's a capital idea!" Clarence cut in. "We'll see you off to the end of our research area, and then follow you a bit further."

"Better yet," Edgar said, "why don't we travel with them? This cat is the first real evidence we've found. Maybe we are just out of their range. We can pack light and see what's further into the jungle."

If Rick's day-trip invitation registered as a bad idea, Edgar's joint expedition response moved the needle up to horrendous.

"The more the merrier," Carlos said. "And a few more eyes on the lookout for jaguars wouldn't hurt."

"Jolly good!" Clarence's face was alive with excitement as he stood up. "Edgar, let's get what we need packed tonight before it gets dark so we are ready to leave at first light."

Edgar nodded and the two of them left the firepit and began to pack up some gear.

Rose turned to Rick and Carlos. "What just happened there?"

"We recruited some help from people who already know the area," Rick said.

"They may know the area, but we don't know them," Rose said.

"I think we do," Rick said. "They're a couple of egghead scientists doing cat research. They couldn't be more harmless."

"Sure, Rose," Carlos said. "I've seen plenty of disreputable people in my day."

Rose mimed shock. "No! Say it isn't so!"

"Anyway," Carlos continued, "Manuel and Geraldo could take care of them if anyone got a crazy idea."

Manuel and Geraldo sat by the firepit, licking their plates. Knowing Carlos' men were ready to resort to violence wasn't as comforting as Carlos intended it to sound.

Rick put his arm around Rose's shoulder and gave her a squeeze. "These two are like us being dealt a pair of aces when we already held two. That's the kind of hand you can bet on."

Rose frowned. No matter how benign they appeared, Rose thought Clarence and especially Edgar were much more like wild cards than aces.

CHAPTER EIGHT

From its perch in the tree, the jaguar had a perfect view of the newcomers' camp. The darkness of the jungle night was near absolute, broken only by the low fire burning in the pit between the tents. What he saw he did not like. Tonight, there were many more humans in the camp, and three slept by the fire. What distressed the jaguar even more was that the scent of one of his brothers came from the table by the tents. The body was gone, but he could still smell the blood. These humans had killed one of his own.

His first reaction was to attack, to exact vengeance for murdering another Night Guardian. He could maim the three by the fire before any were awake enough to react. This jungle could only have one apex predator, and the intruders needed to learn that mankind was not to be it.

But the master would not abide such an action. It would conflict with the Sacred Edict, the imperative embedded into the jaguar's instinct at the moment of its transformation: *Serve the master*. His duty was to report. The master would decide when and how to avenge the jaguar's brother's death.

As soon as he could hear the drone of the humans sleeping, he leapt down from the branch, landing in near silence on his padded feet. At the base of the tree, the peccary he'd hunted and tranquilized earlier lay beside a log. The jaguar picked it up in its mouth as gently as it would a jaguar cub. He sniffed the air for the master's scent, then headed into the jungle.

He followed one of the hunting paths he and his brothers frequented. It wound around hills and rocks and crossed a stream over a fallen tree. The peccary twitched in his jaws. The jaguar injected a few more drops of venom and the little pig went still.

Soon he was back among the giant stone blocks the humans had stacked in the time before his transformation. In the ages since then, the jungle had worked hard to reclaim its territory, and now trees grew out of the buildings and dirt and scrub covered the avenues between them. He trotted down one of those former streets to the largest building in the complex. The stepped pyramid rose several hundred feet high. At the time of his transformation, the temple had been a showplace, polished and painted. A squad of slaves kept it swept clean. Now it was a tangle of vines and plant life, looking more like a hill than a sacred temple. Leaves vibrated from the rustle of the rats as they scurried where supplicant priests once prayed.

One temple adornment had defied the elements. A gleaming band of silver encircled the temple's base. After the Great Battle, the intruders in the metal shells had hammered the long strips into the stone, and the city had gone silent.

The jaguar trotted around the temple to the pyramid's side. Centuries of comings and goings of the Night Guardians had kept the encroaching jungle at bay here. A square opening to a horizontal ventilation shaft beckoned. The decorative stone grill that had covered the shaft was long gone.

The jaguar trotted up to the opening. It was only a few feet square and he had to drop the peccary into the shaft first, then crouch down into the shaft and crawl forward on his belly, pushing the little pig with his nose. Ages of doing so had left a slick coating of animal body oils over the shaft floor.

Eventually, he reached the end of the shaft. He nudged his head against the stone wall blocking the end. It slid aside to reveal a dimly lit corridor near the pyramid's center. He pushed the peccary out and it dropped several feet down onto a stone floor. The jaguar crawled forward and jumped down after it.

With the peccary again secure in his jaws, the jaguar trotted to the end of the corridor. It opened to a large room in the center of the pyramid. Overhead, a crystal orb lit the room in a soft glow, aided by a string of burning lamps along the wall.

An altar sat in the center of the room. The jaguar bounded over to it, rested his front paws atop it, and then dropped the peccary on the slab. Then the cat backed away to the corridor and waited.

In moments, the Master appeared on the stairway across from the corridor. A long, red cape draped over his shoulders and a hood hid most of his face in shadows, though the pale ghostly bit of it visible was gaunt and decidedly not quite human. He descended the steps with deliberation. When he reached the floor, he turned to the jaguar.

"You're late," the Master growled. The Master communicated telepathically and it always sounded like his voice came from within the jaguar's head.

Before the jaguar could respond, the Master spied the peccary offering on the altar. He dove on it and opened his mouth wider than any human ever could. A pair of long, curved canine teeth protruded from his upper jaw. He bit down on the peccary's neck.

But he did not tear the animal apart. The animal shuddered as the Master drank the blood that surged through the creature's severed artery. The poor creature visibly shrank as the Master drained every drop of blood from its body. When finished, he discarded the corpse at the jaguar's feet. The big cat would eat what the Master had not.

The Master wiped his mouth with the back of his hand. Muscles swelled all across his body. His skin went from a death-like gray to a brighter white. He let out a satisfied growl.

Then the jaguar felt the Master's presence in his mind. The force of it weighed so heavily upon him that he was mentally helpless. He stared glassy-eyed at nothing as his memories of the past day replayed in his head. When they finished, the Master withdrew and the jaguar felt like he'd just surfaced from an underwater swim.

"Watch the intruders." The command rang inside the jaguar's head.

The jaguar retrieved the peccary and left the room. In a few moments, he was back outside the temple with a new mission.

But false dawn already lit the horizon, and Night Guardians only prowled between sunset and sunrise. He would return to his den. When the sun set again, he would, as always, follow the Master's orders.

CHAPTER NINE

As dawn broke, Ocotlan left the village to begin observing the intruders. He carried an atlatl, a two-foot-long S-shaped stick. One end had a grip, the other a cup to seat a projectile. The red sash designating him the tribe's First Warrior wrapped the handle. Other warriors may have preferred a bow and arrow or a sling, but the atlatl was Ocotlan's weapon of choice. He'd personally carved and tested it, and in his hands it could propel a poisoned dart faster than the eye could see. He had a dozen such darts in the pouch at his waist.

He moved through the jungle in silence, as his father had taught him, using techniques passed down through uncountable generations. He chose not just the how of each step he took, but the careful placement. Remaining unobserved as one warrior meant the village remained hidden as many. His skills had earned him the title of First Warrior under Chief Necalli.

Daylight meant he would not encounter the Night Guardians, and that was as it was ordained. It was written that man owned half the day, and the jaguars the other. The Night Guardians prowled the darkness, and any man caught out in it was fair game. Young, foolish warriors had ignored this warning, traveled at night, and never returned.

Ocotlan arrived at his observation tree. He thought of it as his, though the deep gouges along the sides betrayed that the Night Guardians used it as well. Did they also know that these intruders needed to be watched? He knew a jaguar could not think as a man, but he also knew that the Night Guardians were no ordinary jaguars.

Ocotlan scaled the tree and settled in at the crook of one of the larger branches. In the clearing ahead stood the two tents the intruders had set up with the firepit between them. The two white men had been here for many lunar cycles, crashing through the jungle with the noise of a peccary herd. But they had stayed close to their camp, and threatened neither the village nor the sacred place. So Ocotlan had kept his poisoned darts in his pouch and the people under watch.

Today was different. Another tent had joined the first two. There were five newcomers to the camp, one of them female with hair the color of fire. This was intriguing, but the other thing he observed was alarming. One of the original intruders stood at the table cutting on the severed head of a Night Guardian.

The desecration sent a shiver through Ocotlan's body. The Night Guardians were the personal servants of Itztli, not to be touched, not to be impeded. To attack one was to sign one's own death sentence.

Even more distressing was the fact that the intruders succeeded. The black jaguars were more powerful than any man and agile enough to avoid arrows and darts. To kill one the intruders must have a powerful weapon or some kind of magic spell. Either would be a threat to the village. Could they also be a threat to Itztli?

That would be something for Necalli, the village chief, to decide.

Ocotlan dropped from the tree. He paused to see if his movement had garnered a reaction from the intruders, but there was none. They were too busy talking among themselves. He grabbed his atlatl and retraced his steps back to the village.

Once well-clear of the intruder's camp, he sprinted the rest of the way home. He arrived to see other villagers milling about the collection of palm-thatched huts. He darted between them until he reached the hut of Necalli. He burst in to find the old man sitting on a mat wearing a simple loincloth, drinking a cup of ātōle.

Necalli was a decade older than Ocotlan. In his prime as First Warrior, none could match him, not even Ocotlan today. But the man had grown paunchy being chief, spending more time eating than hunting the food he ate.

Necalli looked up, clearly displeased. "Ocotlan, you are supposed to be observing the intruders."

"I was and have to report what I've seen. The newcomers have killed one of the Night Guardians. Beheaded it and were desecrating the head."

Necalli's eyes narrowed. "That cannot stand."

"Even worse, there are more of them now. All are white."

The chief thought a moment. "Take warriors and return to their camp."

Ocotlan smiled. "I will make certain no intruder survives."

"No! Observe them. Shadow their movements."

Ocotlan could not believe what the chief said. The old man had indeed spent too much time away from the hunt. These people needed to be killed. "You would let them desecrate the Sacred Place?"

"If they approach the Sacred Place, intervene. Capture them and bring them back to the village."

Before he said something that got him demoted from First Warrior, Ocotlan nodded and left the hut. It was all he could do to keep from screaming in frustration. The right course of action was so clear to see. Necalli had never ordered a life taken. Was he even capable of it?

Ocotlan was certain that when he became chief, he'd bring that warrior spirit back to his people.

***

Necalli rested on a chair in the corner. Ocotlan had brought him troubling news.

The first two intruders had arrived by canoe, and had raised his curiosity. Only in the stories of the elders did white people exist. In the generations that his tribe had guarded the Sacred Place, the only outsiders had been lost members of neighboring tribes, and even those had become so rare that neither he nor his father had ever encountered one. His people no longer believed the myth of Quetzalcoatl, that a fair-skinned god would return to lead them. Instead, all knew the story of Cortez and the Spanish, white men who came to destroy and enslave them. So, Necalli had ordered his warriors to watch these intruders and observe their bizarre ways of living and the strange garments that covered their bodies.

Once they had set up their camp, the newcomers seemed to do nothing. They planted no crops, built no true homes, hunted just the barest amount to survive. In the same way his people observed them, these men observed the jungle, walking and making marks on thin, white sheets like bark shavings.

Necalli's people often made temporary camps elsewhere in the dry season to harvest maize in the receding waters, and then returned to the village before the rains began. He had wondered if the two intruders would do the same. He feared a confrontation with these newcomers and hoped they would soon return to their homes and keep him from having to make the decision to eject them, or worse.

But they had not left.

Then came the roaring along the river, like some great beast released from the earth by the gods, and now there were more intruders and one was female. The only reason to add females to a camp was to add children and make it permanent. That meant the intruders would expand, inevitably find Necalli's people, and then threaten Itztli and the Sacred Place. They had already taken the first step and killed a Night Guardian. And it could not be a coincidence that these intruders arrived on the eve of the annual offering to Tezcatlipoca.

Necalli could not put off taking action any longer. The signs were clear and the situation would only worsen from here.

His tenure as chief had been shaky recently. The rains had been delayed and the jungle had not provided as it always had. A strange, red algae had bloomed in the river last month and then dead fish littered the riverbanks for a week. That had started grumblings among the people about whether Necalli had the favor of Tezcatlipoca. Then when he'd let the intruders' camp on the edge of tribal lands, some of the younger warriors had taken that as a sign of weakness. His father had warned him on the day of his ascension that there would always be someone ready to topple a leader who could not deliver for his people.

According to the sun, it was the time of the annual sacrifice, and the intruders must not interfere with it. Ocotlan's poison darts might have to deal with the intruders.

CHAPTER TEN

The morning hadn't brought any relief from the jungle's oppressive atmosphere. Rose had hoped that like most places she'd been, the night would bring cooler temperatures and perhaps a breeze, but neither had happened. Now as the sun filtered through the canopy, she was certain that it would only get hotter and more humid throughout the day. She doubted wherever they were going to pitch camp tonight would be any better.

She gripped the tent pole so she could drop the tent and paused. She checked again for the sensation she'd felt earlier, that feeling that she was being watched from somewhere in the jungle. It was gone now for certain, but she was just as certain that it had been there before, and that she'd heard some movement among the plants at the same time. She wasn't about to dismiss her observations as paranoia-induced, brought on by Clarence and Edgar catching a giant jaguar.

She removed the tent pole and the canvas tent collapsed to the ground. Rick stepped up to her side and began to help her fold it up.

"You looked concerned just now," Rick said.

She considered telling him the truth about her sensation of being watched. She dismissed the idea, certain that Rick would just gloss over her concerns anyway. "That was me still smelling the remains of Clarence's jaguar dissection."

"That did have a special stink to it. But that wasn't what was bothering you. Confess. It's good for the soul."

"I don't think we're alone out here," she said.

Rick looked alarmed. "You saw someone?"

"Maybe. I definitely felt like there was someone out there watching us before, but not now. I know you'll dismiss it as my imagination."

"Just the opposite," Rick said. "I think that the dangerous situation here has heightened your senses, and you did get a feel for something out there. It might have been a person. More likely it had been some curious animal. But it's just more proof that we need to keep our wits about us on this little hike."

"Thanks, Rick."

Rick drew his machete from his belt. "Why, just let some animal try and threaten my wife. I'll chop and dice it like a French chef."

Rose smiled. "What do you know about French cooking?"

"Tons. I eat french fries all the time."

Rick returned his machete to his belt and the two of them folded and packed the tent. Carlos gave Manuel and Geraldo all their directions. Rose did not understand the conversation, but it seemed they were less than excited about their roles as pack mules. She didn't want to think about their reactions if the lost City of Gold still remained lost by the time the group decided to head home.

A half hour later, everyone was packed and the group headed out. Clarence only carried a notebook, but Edgar had his rifle slung across a shoulder.

Rose whispered in Rick's ear. "The only armed person here is a total stranger."

"If another jaguar shows up," Rick said, "you'll be glad he's here with that rifle. By the time I could defend us with a machete from a jaguar attack, it would be way too late."

Carlos shot a compass heading in the direction the map said the lost city lay. "It should be out there."

"Been out in this direction before, Professor?" Rick asked.

Clarence scratched his chin. "A little ways. Flat ground for the most part, but the jungle gets dense as the land rises out of the flood plain."

"That's good news," Rick said. "It would take a lot of trees to keep the city hidden. Off we go."

Leave it to Rick to think hacking through a jungle would be good news, Rose thought.

Clarence's description turned out to be dead on. The ground was flat and the jungle grew gradually denser. They struggled through thick stands of green, then made up a little time on some more open spaces. The men started a rotation taking the lead so that when one got tired of the regular pauses for cutting and chopping, a fresh set of arms could take his place. Carlos kept an eye on their compass heading and Rose was glad he did. With the sunlight filtered by the canopy, she had no idea which direction they were heading.

After one particularly tough slog through a barricade of thick vines, another more open stretch appeared. Rose stepped into it with relief. Then her foot caught on something a few inches high. She fell face first and barely had time to get her hands out to catch her fall. She landed with a fraction of an inch between her nose and the ground.

The group paused and Rick dashed over. "Are you all right?"

"Yes, I just tripped."

As Rose raised herself up, she noticed the ground under her palms felt very hard and flat. She went to her knees and with both hands pried away a layer of accumulated dirt and ground cover. She revealed a flat, gray stone.

"That's strange," Clarence said.

"No," Rose said. "It's impossible. Look at the marks on it. This stone was carved."

She pulled away more ground clutter and revealed several more similar stones.

"A floor?" Clarence said.

Rose looked right and left. There was significant plant encroachment, but there was also a distinct line through the jungle with no trees on it.

"There's a path. These stones aren't a floor. They're part of a road, like the Romans used to make."

Rick dropped down beside her and swept and pulled until he exposed even more paving stones. "You're right."

Rose spun around to check the area where she'd tripped. A low hump ran along the edge of the discovered roadway. She swept clear the part where she'd tripped and revealed another stone, this one more like a brick. It was mortared to others that ran along the road edge like a curb.

"This road is better built than the one to the village where I grew up," Carlos said.

Rick studied the road edge and then his eyes went wide. "It's more than just nicely built."

He pulled his machete from his belt and knelt down beside Rose. He scraped clean the top of the next brick in the curb and revealed a gleaming inlay of gold.

"What the hell?" Edgar said.

Everyone gathered around the brick. Rick struck the stone around the inlay's edges with the base of his machete. Bits flaked and chipped. Then using the tip of the blade, he popped the gold out into the palm of his hand. He held it out and everyone gathered around. The sunlight made the surface glitter.

"And, jackpot," Rick whispered.

"Why would someone waste gold like that?" Clarence said.

"The Aztecs did not value gold like the Spaniards did," Rose said. "They only thought of it as useful for decorations, jewelry."

"Still," Clarence said, "who decorates a road like that?"

"That's no decoration," Carlos said. "Maybe it's like landing lights on a runway. Reflected moonlight on the gold would mean you could see the road in the dark."

"Sure," Rose said. "And when the river floods, if it was underwater, the gold might still sparkle when the sun hit it."

Carlos picked up the ingot from Rick's palm and examined it. "It also isn't gold. This is pyrite. Fool's gold they call it."

Disappointment crossed Edgar's face. "Are you certain?"

"Positive. Learned the difference early on. You'd be surprised how many people try to pass off pyrite as gold in my line of work."

An *honor among thieves* comment occurred to Rose but she kept it to herself.

"I hate to bring this up," she said, "but this discovery may explain something, and not in a way we want it to. What if the Spaniards did mistake this pyrite for gold? And what if the city with 'streets made of gold' was a corruption of 'a road lined with gold'?"

Carlos bounced the pyrite up and down on his palm. "That would mean we took a long trip for a cache of fool's gold."

Rick sagged, but then straightened up and took a deep breath. "We can't think that way. People found gold in Aztec cities all over Mexico. We'll find this lost city, and discover even more gold. Is the myth embellished? Probably it is. But cut those claims in half, and it's still a fortune. We can't give up now that we found the shortcut."

"Shortcut?" Edgar said.

"The compass bearing we were following was the general direction of the city based on our map. I'll lay three-to-one that this road will take us there. Where else would it go but from the river to the city?"

"Much as I hate to admit when my husband has a good point," Rose said, "I think he's right."

Rick smiled at Rose. "See how good it feels to say that? Admitting that all the time would work wonders for you."

Rose rolled her eyes.

"Carlos," Rick said, "you keep that pyrite as a down payment on the real gold to come. Now, let's find that city."

CHAPTER ELEVEN

After several hundred years, the abandoned Aztec road was worse for the wear. Nowhere was the stone that created it visible. A patchwork of silt, earth, and creeping vegetation worked hard to keep the hand-hewn pavers hidden. But it still created a general path through the jungle, even if there were spots where trees had burst through in a victory for nature over civil engineering.

The group did make far better time along this route. It gave Rose hope that if indeed the city was close, they might get there before nightfall. She would certainly prefer to set up camp in the ruins of a city than in the wilds of the jungle.

"I have to mention something I find a bit strange," Clarence said. "There are no animal tracks along our route. As an open, flat trail, such a road would literally be the path of least resistance. Small animals would naturally select it, and then predators would patrol it. I see no signs of either."

"Spot on," Edgar said. "Seems we're the first creatures to use this road since the Aztecs."

"What do you think that means?" Rose said.

"It means," Clarence said, "that whatever perceived risk the creatures associate with the road is greater than the energy and time spent smashing through the jungle. We should be wary."

"Or, it's just the opposite," Rick said. "If the predators aren't here, this is the safest place we can be. Let's keep it moving!"

A few minutes later, they came across some mossy lumps in the otherwise relatively flat ancient roadway. As the group stepped around them, Rose noticed a flat, metal tong protruding from one.

"One moment." She knelt down, grabbed the edge, and pulled up.

A Spanish conquistador's helmet came up out of the dirt. It was egg-shaped, with an upswept brim in the front and rear and a comb that ran along the helmet's crest. Rose brushed the dirt away and revealed a polished surface with engravings in Spanish along the comb.

"Wow!" Rick went to Rose and took the helmet from her hands. "Look at this. Did I tell you we were on the right track? Proof that the conquistadors were here."

"That can't be," Edgar said as he shook his head, "iron helmets would have rusted away centuries ago. How can a legitimate one still be here?"

Rick handed it back to Rose. "Is it the real thing?"

Rose blew more dirt from the helmet and gave it a closer look. "It looks authentic. The reason it's still here is it's made of silver, or at least clad in it."

"That seems like a pretty expensive way to make a helmet," Carlos said.

"I can't believe there were silversmiths who knew how to make such things," Clarence said.

"I've seen armor and weapons in museums made of precious metals," Rose said, "even adorned with expensive gems, but they were for ceremonial use."

Everyone went to uncover a different lump in the roadway. When they were finished, they'd unearthed a collection of Spanish-era body armor. Manuel uncovered a helmet, brushed it off and put it on his head. Geraldo struck it with the base of his machete. The impact made a deep clang. Manuel teetered back and forth and Geraldo laughed.

Everything they uncovered was made of silver. Edgar's blasé attitude about doing research evaporated and he showed some enthusiasm for the first time as he buffed the breastplate in his hands.

The breadth of the find stunned Rose. This was an antique dealer's dream come true.

"This armor is something only royalty could afford," she said, "and there wasn't anyone with that kind of social rank in Mexico in the sixteenth century."

Carlos took the helmet from Rose's hands and inspected the lettering engraved on it. "This inscription says the helmet was blessed by the Cardinal of Madrid to fight against the demons of darkness."

"Then these conquistadors were financed by someone with money and religious connections," Rose said.

"Even more reason to not bring it out here and dump it on the road to an Aztec city," Rick said.

"Perhaps it wasn't dumped," Clarence said. "A more gruesome explanation would be that it was worn, and the soldiers wearing it met their fate right here. The armor survives, but the bodies and clothes are long gone."

Rick looked over the breastplate in his hand. "There's no battle damage here, nor on the other pieces."

"The natives were quite skilled with poisoned arrows and darts," Clarence said, "maybe skilled enough to land the points in vulnerable spots between the armor."

"A sad story we won't ever know for sure," Edgar said, "but the good part is, these are worth some serious pounds sterling. Am I right?"

"Most definitely," Rose said.

"I'm guessing enough to pay for renting my plane," Carlos said.

"And then some."

"We'd waste a full day if we lug it back to the campsite," Rick said. "We'll stash it here and pick it up on the way back to the plane. I'm going to go out on a limb and say that no one will wander by and steal it."

"There isn't a soul around for over a hundred miles," Edgar said.

They made a pile of the armor under a large tree by the side of the old roadway to make finding it all again easier.

"See, Rosie?" Rick said. "This trip has already paid for itself. Of course, this is just a rounding error compared to the gold we'll find in the city, but it proves I was right about this adventure."

Rose looked him in the eyes. "Let's turn around. We have these pieces. They'll turn a profit, get us some great recognition, bring us more buyers and sellers. As you would put it, we'd walk away winners."

"And leave a huge pot on the table while we hold four of a kind? Not on your life."

"We have no idea what we're walking into up ahead."

"Sure we do. The City of Gold." Rick flicked a finger against the helmet in her hand. "These trinkets here will set us up for a few months, but a city full of gold will set us up for life, and it's all going to waste sitting undiscovered at the end of this road. Imagine the artifacts there. We can't quit now."

Rick's eagerness had an annoying habit of being infectious. This moment was no exception. Rose felt her commonsense idea to quit while they were ahead fade away under the bright light of Rick's vision of their quest's conclusion. Rose set down the helmet atop the pile and followed Rick as he headed down the road.

CHAPTER TWELVE

Rick's boundless enthusiasm might have been infectious, but the symptoms didn't last long. The further they made their way down the old road, the less enchanted Rose was with the plan to risk it all by pushing on to the lost city.

Rick led the way in that fearless mode he assumed when he was making a big bet, certain he'd come up a winner, often in spite of the odds. Manuel followed right behind him. Edgar had worked his way up the group from near the rear with his father until he was alongside Rose.

"Are you and your husband out and about like this often?" he asked.

"More often than I'd like," she said. "Most of our antiques are acquired in far more mundane ways. What about you? How long have you worked with your father?"

"I really don't. This is a one-time thing. I was between jobs and, just as he was leaving for this research trip, his assistant fell ill. He planned on pushing off alone. Bloody old hardhead wouldn't admit how foolhardy that idea was. For his own sake, I volunteered to accompany him."

"So, you haven't done field work before?"

"Heavens, no. I work in banking and finance. Fleet Street and all that. Quite frankly, I had no idea what I was getting into."

Rose smiled. She was embarrassed that she'd been suspicious of Edgar and his father. "It seems we never do either."

"You're sure there's a City of Gold out there?"

"I'm sure there once was. We'll have to see what's still standing."

"Your husband mentioned an aeroplane. That's how you got here?"

"A flying boat that landed on the river."

"A smarter choice than the small boat we took to get up here. Maybe we can get a ride back with you."

"Do you think he'll be done with his research?"

"I'll talk him into that," Edgar said.

Up ahead, a dead animal lay on the path. The group slowed and bunched up behind Rick. When Rose got up to her husband, she recognized it as a peccary. The dun-colored, pig-like creature looked to weigh about twenty pounds. Chunks of flesh looked burned away, with the edges of the wounds charred. Thick, silvery threads wrapped around the corpse.

"Looks like that pig went down fighting," Carlos said.

Rick touched a finger to the silver thread. The thread stuck to him. He recoiled, and after an inch of stretch, the thread snapped back against the peccary.

"That's strange," Clarence said. "If it wasn't so thick, that would pass for spider webbing."

Rose glanced around them. Indeed, overhead to the left an enormous spiderweb stretched between the trunks of two palms. It was at least twelve feet across and just as high. At one angle, it was almost invisible, but if she rotated her view a bit, she could make out the entire, perfect structure. It wasn't just the size that was larger than normal. The silk and the pattern was also proportionally larger.

This wasn't an oversized web made by a small spider. It was an enormous web spun by a huge spider.

"Look out!" Clarence cried out.

A giant spider plummeted down from the tree canopy, trailing a thread of silk behind it. The main body was the size of a softball, but the abdomen was larger than a dinner plate. Its eight legs spread out wide, each measuring a foot-and-a-half long. The spider's glossy, black finish carried a red hourglass shape on the abdomen that Rose immediately recognized.

This was a black widow spider.

She'd seen them all the time around Savannah, but those were thumbnail-sized. If those versions were painfully poisonous, these Mexican behemoths were likely instantly fatal.

The spider dropped onto Manuel. It landed on his shoulder and the man screamed. He pushed at the spider to dislodge it, but it hung on tight. Its abdomen swayed and it sprayed a mass of webbing on Manuel's hands, sticking them together. Then the spider reared back its head, opened its mouth, and then sank its fangs into the man's back. His wail of panic turned into a shriek of pain.

Manuel whirled and jerked as he flailed his arms against the spider. The creature bit him again.

Edgar brought his rifle to bear, but his aim danced right and left as Manuel's spinning and jerking didn't offer a clean shot.

Manuel hit the ground. Rick gripped his machete with both hands and charged the prone man. He struck the spider twice, but the blade just bounced off the spider's hard body.

Manuel cried out a final time, and then collapsed. The spider raised its head to face the others and hissed. It scrambled across the ground toward Rose.

Edgar's rifle barked. Its bullet struck the spider's head. It exploded in a splash of black goo. The spider dropped to the ground and went still. Geraldo stepped over and poked it with his machete. Carlos knelt at Manuel's side. He checked for a pulse and then shook his head.

"That was close," Rick said.

"Rick!" Rose pointed up the path.

Several yards away, three more spiders drifted down from the canopy. They landed on the ground and began a rapid crawl toward the group.

Edgar aimed at one and pulled the trigger. The gun clicked and jammed. Edgar cursed and fought against the frozen rifle bolt.

"Let's get out of here," Carlos said.

The group turned to head back down the trail. Three more spiders already blocked the way and were crawling in their direction. Leaves overhead rustled and promised that still more waited in the wings.

The group backed into a natural defensive circle. Clarence dropped his notebook and made a panicked dash for the jungle.

"Father, no!" Edgar shouted.

But Clarence kept going and was soon lost in the foliage. A spider dropped down from the trees between the group and where Clarence vanished.

"Bloody coward," Edgar grumbled.

The men readied their machetes to defend themselves. Edgar held his rifle by the barrel, prepared to use it as a club.

Rose grabbed a cast iron pan that hung from the side of Carlos' pack. She raised it over her shoulder. The pan wouldn't save her life, but she was going to go down swinging.

New spiders appeared at each end of the path. They began to leap from tree to tree, leaving behind a thick strand of webbing. The new black widows were building a fence, making sure none of their victims escaped. As they did, the six on the path closed to within a few feet of the group.

The group backed up until their shoulders touched.

"I'd tell you I loved you," Rick said, "but that would sound like I didn't think we were going to get out of this alive."

"If we do," Rose said, "I'm hitting you with this pan."

The advancing spiders hissed. The arachnids among the trees finished two-thirds of the gossamer corral.

Clarence reappeared with an armful of large, green fruit. They were shaped like pears and had a pattern of thorns across the skin. He bolted through a gap in the spider fence and rolled all but one of them at the group. They bounced against people's feet.

Clarence stopped short of the group. He tore open his fruit and exposed a soft, creamy white flesh with large black seeds. With one hand, he scooped out some of the fruit and threw it on the ground in front of some approaching spiders. It splattered and the spiders instantly stopped. Then the three scampered backward.

Clarence scooped out another handful and tossed it at the other advancing spiders. This glob hit the ground and some splashed on one of the creatures. That spider screamed, shook, and ran off. The other two backed away a few yards from the huddle of scared humans.

"Cut those guanabanas open!" Clarence ordered. He threw bits of the fruit at the fence-spinning spiders. When struck, each one abandoned its mission. "Hit the spiders."

Rose dropped her frying pan and picked up a thorny fruit. She dug her nails into the surface and pulled. The skin ripped open and released a smell like pineapples and oranges. She stuck two fingers into the gooey flesh and then sent a glob at one of the black widows. It missed but landed in front of the arachnid with a splat. The spider recoiled and then scampered back to the jungle.

All around her, the others did the same. The strange fruit broke up the spider attack. The creatures retreated off the path or back into the trees.

Rose looked at Clarence, incredulous. "What did we just do?"

"Spiders dislike citrus," Clarence said. "The guanabanas may not technically be citrus, but they have a lot of citrus attributes. I took a chance that it would be enough to send the spiders packing, and it did."

Carlos poked out a blob with a finger and put it in his mouth. "Mmm. And it doesn't taste bad."

"Completely edible. Just avoid the black seeds. Those are quite toxic."

Clarence took a tent pole from a pack and headed for the spider his son had shot. Rose went to check on Manuel. Geraldo joined her. He looked down on his dead comrade with sadness.

The man's skin was already gray, his body lifeless. On his back, his shirt was torn around two wounds where the spider had bitten him. Though the spider hadn't torn the flesh from the man's body, the wounds were deep and wide, and strangely blackened instead of bloody. The myth of monsters in the jungle clearly wasn't all myth.

Carlos stepped up and put his arm around Geraldo's shoulder. He said something in Spanish in a comforting tone.

Clarence prodded the spider with the pole, flipping it over and examining the legs. "*Latrodectus mactans*. Commonly called a black widow, though I must say that this one is of an immense size, much larger than any spider on Earth."

"Manuel's wounds look horrible," Rose said.

"Yes, spiders like this deliver a neurotoxin. At this size and concentration, this species' toxin seems to also be quite corrosive. I'm afraid that after the first bite, this poor chap was doomed."

"We'll be the same if we keep going," Carlos said. "One tossed blob of mush misses, and a spider will do that to us."

"And black widows are quite territorial," Clarence said. "We can expect a reception like this whenever we meet one."

"What if we use the guanabana like insect repellent?" Rick said. "Spread it on ourselves?"

"Capital idea," Clarence said. "That should work."

"Should?" Rose said.

"Most likely," Clarence said.

Rick rubbed a bit of the creamy fruit between his fingers. "This is probably good for your skin, Rosie. If it doesn't work, at least you'll go out glowing like a Hollywood starlet."

"Remember that promise I made about the frying pan?" Rose said.

Rick feigned fear and took a step back.

Rose dipped her fingers into the fruit and began to apply it to her skin. It did have a consistency like a rather thick lotion, and she couldn't complain about the fruity scent. That part could have certainly been worse.

She noticed Rick wrinkle his nose as he rubbed a glob on his neck. "Problem, Rick?"

"I'm not used to smelling like a fruit cocktail."

"This may be the beginning of a whole new fragrance direction for you."

"Don't bet on it."

Clarence and Edgar went into the jungle, returned with a few more guanabanas, and the crew packed them for future use.

"Those spiders might have been what killed those conquistadors way back when," Rick said. "That would account for the armor still being in the road."

"And the plant that could have saved them was probably growing a few yards away," Rose said.

"Do you want to do something for Manuel?" Rick said to Carlos.

"We'll bury him on the way back," Carlos said.

He and Geraldo grabbed the corpse's arms and legs, and moved it off to the side of the path. Carlos made the sign of the cross, uttered some prayers, and crossed himself again. Then the two rejoined the group.

Geraldo took a machete to the spider webbing that blocked their path forward. It did not cut easily, but it did part. The group shouldered their packs and headed down the trail in a cloud of sweet perfume.

Ahead and overhead, a black widow hung to a branch.

Rick brought his machete to the ready. "Spider ahead. Stay sharp."

As the group approached, it descended on a silvery thread. Rose's pulse quickened.

Halfway down, the spider shuddered and made a distressed-sounding hiss. It scrambled back up the strand of web and vanished in the canopy.

Rick beamed. "There you go, we are spider-proof. Now it's going to be clear sailing all the way to the City of Gold."

Rose wished that was true, but she didn't think they could be that lucky.

CHAPTER THIRTEEN

Geraldo took the lead as the group continued up the decayed Aztec highway. Everyone moved slower now as they had proof-positive they needed to be wary. Rick wasn't going to say it, but if they'd already encountered giant jaguars and huge spiders, he was afraid that something even worse might be waiting just around the next corner.

The jungle was alive with sound. Birds screeched from far and near, lead solos over a chorus of insect trills and chirps. The noise put Rick even more on edge, though he guessed that having them all suddenly fall silent would be ominous and much worse.

Out of the corner of his eye, he thought he saw a set of ferns off the trail sway back and forth, then heard the scamper of feet. He was about to write it off as imagination when he heard Rose's voice.

"Don't tell me you didn't see that."

It seemed the motion in the woods hadn't been his overactive imagination. He wished it had been.

"Seemed like there was something out there," he admitted.

"Something," Rose said, "or *somethings*, and they've been following us since the spider attack."

"Curious animals, maybe," Rick said.

"Every animal we've encountered so far wants to kill us, so that doesn't make me feel any better."

Rick didn't have any comforting rejoinder he could add to that. She was right. He just kept following Geraldo, with his head on a swivel watching for whatever it was out there that might have been shadowing them.

Up ahead on the path, a man sprinted out of the jungle to block their way. He was about five feet tall with toned muscles and a bowl haircut that only went halfway down to his ears. His skin was a golden brown, and Rick could see a lot of it because all the man wore was a loincloth. The sight would be comical if the man wasn't carrying an S-shaped weapon with a large, sharp dart nested in one end. Rick wasn't exactly sure how it worked, but he was completely sure he did not want to find out.

The group stopped. Rick stepped back to put himself between the man and Rose. Geraldo drew his machete and stared hard at the man.

"Clarence," Rick said, "I thought there weren't any people for a hundred miles."

"It seems I was a bit mistaken. There are rumors of tribes here that haven't had contact with Westerners for centuries, if ever."

"Looks like those aren't rumors," Carlos said.

Edgar raised his rifle and pointed it at the native man.

Rose gasped and pressed the barrel down to the ground. "You can't just shoot him."

The native took a step forward and pointed his weapon at Geraldo.

Geraldo uttered a curse in Spanish and raised his machete to strike a blow.

A small arrow whizzed out of the jungle and struck Geraldo in the chest. He screamed and dropped his machete. He grabbed the arrow with both hands and pulled it out. Rick sighed in relief to see that it had not gone in very deep at all and the man had screamed more in shock than in pain.

Geraldo threw down the arrow. He made a move to pick up his machete, but then a spasm wracked his body. His eyes rolled back into his head and foam bubbled at his lips. Then he fell forward and struck the ground face first. His nose made a sickening crunch, but Geraldo didn't react. He also didn't breathe.

"Arrows tipped in poison," Clarence said. "Fatal if they so much as scratch you."

"And there's who knows how many other archers in the jungle," Rose said.

Rick slowly raised his hands. "Let's not make any moves that will upset these people."

Everyone raised their hands.

Edgar shouldered his rifle and did the same. He turned to Rose. "You should have let me shoot the bastard."

The man with the dart-thrower uttered several sentences in a strange tongue. Rick had no idea what he said. But then the warrior pointed the weapon at the group and waved them forward. *That* Rick understood. As the group trudged forward, a native archer appeared on each side of the path. They fell in behind the group with arrows nocked in the bowstrings.

"He's speaking a version of the native dialect," Clarence said. "I picked up some of it before we began our trip upriver. I could understand *chief* and *village*, I think."

"Much better than 'dinner' and 'cannibal' in my book," Rick said.

The three natives took them further down the path they had been following. After a mile or so, the men steered the group off onto a rudimentary trail cut into the jungle. Twenty minutes later, they came to the warriors' village.

The whole collection of huts took up just a few acres. The natives had cleared the smaller plants away to make some space and their huts were scattered among the remaining large trees. Given the quality of construction, Rick doubted that the people living here could have felled those massive trees if they wanted to. The huts were made of mid-sized branches and palm frond thatch. Many of the structures were little more than lean-tos or sagging thatched roofs held aloft by four spindly legs. Fires smoldered in pits within many of the shelters and the scent of charred wood tinged the air.

Scantily clad natives moved between the buildings: men, women, and even a few naked children. As each caught sight of the overburdened prisoners the warriors brought in, they either froze in place or fled in fear. Rick guessed that this was one of those tribes who had never seen people from the outside world.

The warriors stopped them outside one hut. The leader poked at Rick's backpack with his weapon, uttered a curt sentence, and then motioned to the ground. Rick didn't need a translator to figure out what the man meant. He shrugged off his pack and dropped it.

The archers tapped the packs of the others with their bows and everyone followed suit.

The leader reached for Rick's machete. Rick had to restrain himself from grabbing the man's wrist. With a whole village to fight and Rose standing next to a man with a quiver full of poisoned arrows, this was not the time or place to make a stand. He let the man take his machete.

The warrior's eyes went wide as he felt the heft of the metal. He turned its sharpened edge up for inspection.

"I'm guessing they haven't mastered metallurgy," Rick said.

"The seaplane would scare them to death," Carlos said.

"And we'd be on it now if you'd listened to me," Rose said to Rick.

The others dumped their gear and machetes in a pile.

Edgar held his rifle to the last. Rick recognized the look on his face. It was the look of a poker player who held a losing hand, but thought that if he made a bigger bet, somehow he could still win. Those people always lost. But the difference between a poker table and this jungle village was if Edgar decided to start some Wild West-inspired gunplay, it wouldn't just be him that lost.

"Let it go, Edgar," Rick said.

His statement bounced Edgar out of the trance he was in.

"They'll swarm us," Rick continued. "Just set the rifle down. They don't know what it is, and if you don't treat it as special, neither will they. And it may sit right here, where we know where to get it when the time is right."

Edgar grudgingly lay the rifle down against a pack. The warriors pushed the five of them into the hut. Then they closed the door and set a heavy stick across hooks on the outside to keep it shut. The dirt floor had a hard, brown crust. Charcoal coated in animal fat drippings filled a firepit in the center. To the side a small table hugged the wall.

The two archers stayed by the door while the leader headed off, Rick guessed to report their arrival to whoever was in charge.

Rick went to Rose and gave her a hug. She buried her face in his shoulder.

"I'm saving the 'I-told-you-so' for later," she said, "but don't think it isn't coming."

Carlos wrinkled his nose. "I've been off the farm for a long time, but I know a hog pen when I smell one."

"At least they moved them out before they moved us in," Rick said.

Edgar ran a finger across the scarred top of the table. "This isn't a holding pen. It's the slaughterhouse. They probably cooked or smoked the meat over that firepit."

"Slaughterhouse," Carlos said. "That makes me feel much better."

"This will all make for a fascinating research paper," Clarence said. "I wish I was certain I was going to live to write it."

Edgar gave the construction of the hut wall a close inspection. "Well, there's nothing to this wall, or that door, as well. Two of us could bash through it and we'd be out of here."

"That's good news," Rose said. "They don't have a real jail because they aren't used to having real prisoners."

"There's only two of them guarding us," Edgar said. "I say we break out, then I make short work of them with the rifle."

"And then the rest of the tribe swarms us," Clarence said. "That's the kind of thinking that never works out for you."

"Bloody hell," Edgar said. "You saw that half of them are already terrified of us. The boom of the rifle ought to scare off the rest of them."

"And then what?" Rick said. "We hike back with all our baggage, slow sitting ducks for the warriors they will eventually send after us for killing the guards? We'll be dead from poisoned arrows before nightfall."

"And by jaguars if we survive past sunset," Clarence said.

"Spiders will get us before either of those will," Carlos said.

"We have the advantage of knowledge," Rose said. "We can use that to make certain that we seem to be the opposite of what Edgar is recommending, completely harmless. They would have no reason to hurt us, or even hold us."

"Plus, if we get in good with them, they may be able to show us the ruins of Tezpaluca," Rick said. "This could end up being the luckiest thing to happen to us."

"Funny thing, Rick," Edgar said, "I don't feel that lucky right now."

CHAPTER FOURTEEN

The Aeromarine 75's bilge wasn't made to accommodate a man of Humphrey's girth.

Maybe he'd been the right size during his trimmer days as a fighter pilot back when this plane was built. But years and beers had added a few pounds and now it was a tight fit to crawl through the access panel on the passenger cabin deck. But the hull had to be sealed. He and the Sinclairs needed a ride out of this uncharted jungle.

He peered in and shined a flashlight at the keel. A quarter-inch of standing water covered it. He wasn't an expert on flying boats, but he was pretty sure that the "boat" part of the name required the water to all stay on the outside.

He played the beam around the rest of the hull. From inside it was easy to see the joints between the sections of veneer.

"You know," he said to himself, "maybe Rose was right after all about having a plywood airplane."

He soon saw the source of the water. On the right side of the hull, two seams glistened where water seeped in along the joint.

Humphrey thought back to his landing, which he was sure had been soft as peach fuzz. The Aeromarine had been on a runway when they took off. Humphrey wondered if that was because the flying boat already leaked. He wouldn't put it past Carlos to lay the blame for this leak on him and try and chisel some damages out of Humphrey's share of the treasure.

The idea made him smile because he might have done just the same thing.

Humphrey flew jobs that were on the far side of legal, into places that were not quite legitimate airfields, in planes that often lacked all the required maintenance. That meant that his Ford Tri-motor flew with the airplane equivalent of a first aid kit. The box carried most of what he might need to get the plane over any mechanical hiccups along the way.

Hoping Carlos was no different, Humphrey pulled himself out of the bilge and began a hunt through the mechanical room in the center of the plane. He soon discovered an incomplete collection of tools and a bucket full of repair items tucked away behind the central gas tanks. Humphrey sorted through swatches of canvas, cans of shellac, and spare spar support wires until he found what he needed: a jar of pine tar.

This black tar was sticky as hell and completely waterproof. Navies had used it for centuries to protect the hulls of wooden ships from the ravages of the elements at sea. Cheap and effective, he knew it would be Carlos' first choice for emergency repairs.

Humphrey pulled a paintbrush and flashlight from the tool bucket and took the jar over to the bilge. He popped the top. The pine tar smelled like a damper version of Hell and had the consistency of homemade peanut butter, which meant it was a lot runnier than he'd heard it should be. He put the jar in the bilge on the keel, and then slid it down near the splitting seams.

He pondered the different positions he could take in the bilge while applying the tar. Every one of them might have been comfortable for a snake, but none were good for a human being. After careful thought he selected the least painful option, and worked his way into the bilge headfirst.

Once his back touched the keel, his nose missed the underside of the cabin deck by just a few inches.

River water soaked his shirt and pants. His back scraped against the ribs in the hull. The sulphureous stink of the tar seemed to force itself down his nose and throat. He imagined it coating the inside of his lungs and then tried to imagine anything else instead.

He inchwormed his way down the hull on his back, trying to glide over the ribs and failing every time. The leaking seam got closer. He stopped when it lined up with his left shoulder. Humphrey tucked the flashlight under his chin with the beam lighting up the hairline gap.

Water pulsed through the seam. Either the leak looked much worse up close, or it had gotten worse in the short time it took for him to get down to it. Either answer was bad news.

Humphrey couldn't see the tar jar with the deck so close to his body. He set it down by his left side. He realized there wasn't enough room to get his right hand across his chest to paint the seam. So he put the brush in his left hand and then blindly dipped it into the sticky tar. As he lifted it out, he could feel the brush had gotten much heavier. He figured the only way he was going to get this done was to bend at the elbow, swing the brush across his chest, then continue around in an incredibly awkward stretch to touch the brush to the seam.

"Okay, Humpy," he said to himself. "Piece of cake. Let's teach this crack a lesson."

He took a deep breath and then brought the brush up and around. The bristles left a swath of dripped tar from his waist to his neck.

"Son of a…at least it missed my mouth."

Humphrey stretched his hand closer to the crack in the hull. He turned his head to the side for a better look.

The flashlight slipped free.

He whipped his right hand up in time to catch the base of the flashlight with his fingertips. That sent a splash of bilgewater across his face. He sputtered as the rank water assaulted his nose and tastebuds.

"The tar might have tasted better."

With a slow pull, he slid the flashlight back to a better spot between his chin and chest. The repositioned beam gave him a well-lit view of the seeping seam. He slapped at it with the paintbrush and left an uneven layer of tar along part of the crack.

The flow slowed. But he'd missed more of the seam than he'd hit.

"One more shot, Humpy. That'll do it."

He brought the brush back around, dipped it in the can, and made another wide sweep, aiming for the seam.

This motion left another trail of tar in its wake, and this time he could feel the substance ooze through his shirt.

But this time the brush did a better job hitting the mark, and delivered half again as much tar. The leak became a seep.

But he knew he didn't have the dexterity or leverage with his oddly-rotated wrist to seal the crack properly. A very bad idea occurred to him. After a moment, no better one came to take its place.

"Everyone says I have too big a damn mouth. Time to put it to good use."

He grabbed the flashlight with his right hand and kept it pointed at the crack. Then with his left hand, he put the handle of the brush in his mouth the way a dog holds a bone. Only the bone had to taste better. Humphrey tried not to think of everyone and everything that had touched the handle during its sordid lifetime.

With a series of spastic jerks of his head, he moved the brush to spread tar up and down the split in the hull. When he was certain the gag-inducing flavor of the brush and the toxic fumes from the tar were about to incapacitate him, Humphrey stopped and took the brush from his mouth. Then he dared take a close look at his handiwork.

A slather of tar covered the crack as well as an irregular several inches on either side of it. But the seeping had stopped. As the tar dried, the bond would get stronger.

"Michelangelo couldn't have done no better."

He dropped the brush and it splashed into the bilge water. He replaced the top on the tar container, not to preserve the rest as much as to keep him from spilling the remainder on himself.

Something scratched against the exterior of the hull.

Humphrey stopped and listened, hoping the noise had been an echo of one of his own motions.

The sounds returned.

"Hell's bells. Now what?"

Feet-first, he inched his way back to the hatch, seeming to scrape against every possible rough surface on the way. By now his clothing had soaked up so much filthy bilge water he wondered if there'd be any left to pump out. He finally got his head beneath the hatch. He pulled himself up and out to a sitting position. The fresh air felt like an angel's kiss. He took in several deep draughts, then climbed out into the cabin.

Foul water dripped from him onto the deck. A horrible stripe of sticky tar arced across his wide belly and up his body. The pretzel-like positions he'd been forced into had strained his neck and left arm past their normal limits. He'd been less of a mess when he'd been standing in a trench on the Western Front.

The scratching sound on the hull returned. He sighed and walked over to the cabin door. His shoes made squishing noises with each step and he thought about how smart it would have been to have taken them off first.

He stood in the cabin door. After adapting to the gloom of the aircraft's bilge, the sunlight reflecting off the water outside blinded him. He squinted down at the side of the hull.

Ripples bounced all along the plane. Within them the fins and scales flashed as a school of fish churned the water.

Whatever they were doing, Humphrey preferred they didn't. He pounded one foot against the hull over where the fish swarmed.

"There now! Beat it before I deep-fry the bunch of you!"

The fish scattered. A satisfied smile crossed Humphrey's face. It turned to a frown as tiny bits of something floated up to the surface. Humphrey knelt down and scooped some out of the water.

He wasn't very familiar with this plane's details, but the bits looked a lot like the paint on the underside of the hull.

CHAPTER FIFTEEN

Necalli sat outside his hut, facing in the direction of the Sacred Place. His eyes were closed, his mind wide open. If there was ever a time he needed to hear Itztli's guidance, it was now. He clutched the gold jaguar neck collar that lay against his breastbone. This chief's decoration was more than ceremonial. It helped the chief hear Itztli's voice. He listened hard, so hard the silence seemed to roar at him. But Itztli did not answer.

He was not surprised. Itztli was not one to be summoned, he was the one to do the summoning. He spoke to Necalli when he had a need, not when Necalli did.

The tribe ran on traditions, the same traditions that Necalli's father observed, and his fathers before him back to the time when the Sacred Place was the center of the world. But traditions did not answer the questions raised by the newcomers' arrival. Were the intruders here to desecrate the Sacred Place? Were they the vanguard of a force to capture and enslave his people? What if one of them was indeed the foretold return of Quetzalcoatl, the brother of Tezcatlipoca, the promised one the Spaniard was mistaken for? Any of these possibilities could be true, or none of them.

A voice interrupted his thoughts. "Necalli?"

He opened his eyes to see First Warrior Ocotlan standing before him. Necalli knit his brow. Ocotlan should have still been monitoring the intruders. "Why are you back in the village?"

"The intruders were moving toward the Sacred Place. We stopped them after the Spider's Gate and captured most of them. They are in the slaughter hut."

Necalli cringed at how much worse Ocotlan had made the problem of the intruders. "Most of them?"

"Chicahua had to kill one who resisted."

If the newcomers were the return of Quetzalcoatl, killing one of them would infuriate Itztli and even Tezcatlipoca himself. Necalli hoped if that was so he could beg forgiveness.

"What will we do with them?" Ocotlan said.

Indeed, that was Necalli's still-unanswered question, and Itztli was not going to help him with a solution. Necalli stood up.

"I will assess the captives." He entered his hut and donned the brightly-colored, feathered headdress of the chief. Then he donned golden wrist guards. Their inlaid rubies signified his position as the tribe's military authority as well.

If Itztli would not help him, he would have to make the decision on his own, and hope that Itztli would approve.

Necalli led Ocotlan to the slaughtering pen. As soon as the archers on guard saw Necalli they straightened up and began to look nervous. Necalli was glad his reputation for swift punishment for the lazy was still intact. He stopped outside the door.

"Open it," he ordered.

Worry crossed Ocotlan's face. He grunted at the guards and both nocked arrows into their bows. Ocotlan removed the crossbar and opened the door. Necalli stepped inside.

The intruders were almost a foot taller than Necalli's greatest warrior. The tallest one, with the skinny moustache, still had fire in his eyes. Such a man must be the group's leader, so Necalli made a note to keep a close watch on him.

Then Necalli noticed that the one standing behind that man was a woman, with skin as pale as the moon and hair the color of fire. It would be odd for the leader to resort to having a companion so disfigured. But he did seem protective of her. Perhaps the woman was a sickly sister.

Outside the hut, several women rummaged through the intruders' packs. Everything they took out looked completely unfamiliar, but it was obvious that their technology to create them was above what Necalli's people possessed. There were utensils and plates made of metal like his neck collar and wrist guards, but the metal was not gold and it was hard as solid stone. He saw books full of strange, simple writing. There were tools and items he could not begin to fathom the purpose of. Even these people's clothing was made of strange material.

Necalli went to the tallest man. "Why have you come into our lands, so close to the Sacred Place?"

The man did not answer. He just stared at Necalli with a look of superiority on his face. The power and authority of Necalli's headdress, neck collar, and royal wrist guards normally were enough to make anyone cower.

A revelation came to Necalli. *These people are not the emissaries of Quetzalcoatl. These have been sent by Tezcatlipoca to evaluate the annual sacrifice to Itztli.*

Necalli pulled Ocotlan back out of the hut and spoke to him in a hushed tone. "We must make these people our guests."

"Guests? These invaders have to be put to death or more of their people will follow."

"You fool! These are emissaries of Tezcatlipoca."

Ocotlan looked confused.

"They have the skin foretold of the emissaries of Quetzalcoatl. Everything they wear, everything they carry is unlike anything we've ever seen."

"Then why did two of the intruders arrive long ago and never approach the village?"

"The first two were sent to judge how we have cared for the land around the Sacred Place, to test that we would observe them. When that pleased Tezcatlipoca, others arrived to assess the ceremony of Itztli's tribute. Why else would they walk into camp on this very day?"

"But one of them attacked me, and we killed him."

"Another test, to see if our people still had the warrior spirit. You passed that test. Did they not go willingly with you after that, even though they outnumbered you?"

Ocotlan did not look convinced. Necalli did not need him to be, only to be obedient.

"These people are now our guests," Necalli said. "Bring them mats and samples of our best food. Make sure they are comfortable until the Offering ceremony."

"We are to give them the freedom to wander the village?" Ocotlan was incredulous.

The respected First Warrior's stunned response made Necalli second-guess himself. "No, perhaps not. We must be sure they only see the best of our people. Keep them under guard in the hut, but be certain all their needs are met."

Ocotlan seemed only partially mollified. "As you command."

Necalli headed back for his hut. His worries about his position as chief would soon all fade away. Itztli's offering would go as planned and curry favor with Tezcatlipoca. The god's emissaries would sing Necalli's praises and then Tezcatlipoca would bestow a great bounty upon his most favored tribe. What had worried him most, the arrival of the intruders, was about to be the best thing that ever happened to him.

***

In the wake of Necalli's departure, Ocotlan seethed with discontent. The old man was clearly out of his mind to think these people were sent by Tezcatlipoca.

Ocotlan had spent longer with the intruders than the chief, and had walked away unimpressed. Their pale skin was no sign of divinity, just proof that they were a sickly people. They wore clothing too hot and constricting for traversing the jungle, and based on all the baggage they carried, they had no idea how to live off the bounty of the land. Wouldn't emissaries of a god be completely provided for?

Ocotlan looked in through a gap in the hut wall at the captives. They did not act like ones knowing they had the power of a god behind their actions. They looked beaten and frightened. They had come to the land of the Sacred Place unprepared. The jungle had worn them down, and Ocotlan and his warriors had vanquished them without a fight.

Only one of the men did not look defeated. Even now, the tallest among them looked Ocotlan straight in the eyes, daring to consider himself an equal to the tribe's First Warrior.

Ocotlan replaced the cross bar on the door and stepped back to address Chicahua and the other guard. They both had quizzical looks on their faces.

"Did we hear the chief right?" Chicahua asked. "We aren't going to execute the intruders?"

"Those are his orders. The intruders live. For now. Necalli will see he has made a mistake and will correct it."

And if he doesn't, Ocotlan thought, *it will fall to me to correct it for him, and become the new chief.*

***

As the lead warrior walked away, Rose felt relieved. For a moment there, she was certain that the chief was giving the order for the three warriors to put the whole group of them to death. It wasn't until the chief departed and one of the guards locked the door that she was sure they were in the clear, at least for now.

"Well, they didn't kill us," Rick said.

"Even though you were looking at that warrior like you wanted him to start a fight," Rose said.

"I've sat at enough poker tables to know you have to portray strength and confidence to win, no matter what hand you've been dealt. I've also learned how to read the other player, and that chief wasn't even holding a pair of threes, no matter how impressive everything he wore seemed."

"Did you see that hardware around that chap's neck?" Edgar said. "And those wrist guards? All of that was solid bloody gold. Why, the jewels in the wrist guards were worth a fortune all by themselves."

"The Aztec rulers were known to have specific royal garments and adornments," Rose said, "a lot like the Egyptians did."

"And the chief wearing all of that precious metal is more proof we're on track to find the City of Gold," Rick said. "This place is a long way from any mining operations or gold deposits. I'll bet the tribe found that jewelry in the city's ruins."

The bar on the outside of the door scraped as it was moved away. Rose's first thought was that the warriors outside had been given a change of orders, and her situation was about to get very dark. She was stunned when the door opened and an older woman entered. She wore a dun-colored, poncho-like garment and carried a handful of woven mats. She spread the mats out on the ground. As she departed, a teenage girl entered.

The girl wore a short skirt and a brightly-colored top that stopped just above her waist. Silky hair stretched halfway down her back, bound at the base of her neck with a seashell clasp. She carried a plate of fruit and nuts that she set down on the butchering table. After giving everyone a curious inspection, her eyes locked on Rose, and more specifically on Rose's hair.

"I'm guessing she's never seen red hair before," Rick whispered.

"I don't suppose she has." Rose stepped next to the girl and smiled. The girl smiled back. Rose pulled some pins from her hair and let it cascade down. The girl's eyes lit up.

Rose took the girl's hand and placed it on her own hair. The girl twittered at the way it felt. She grinned and looked away, face flushed.

"Look who made a friend," Rick said.

Then the girl took the seashell clasp from her own hair, and handed it to Rose. Rose nodded in gratitude. The girl twittered again, and then scampered out of the hut. The door closed and a warrior replaced the cross bar.

"Things are looking up," Carlos said. "Room service and we didn't even order it."

"What did I tell you?' Rick said. "I read that chief like a book."

"I can't remember the last time you read a book," Rose said.

"I guess they wouldn't try to make us comfortable if they were planning on killing us," Clarence said.

Edgar went to the table, picked up a nut and tossed it into his mouth. "But they did still lock that door, and we won't be finding the City of Gold stuck inside this hut."

"If we play our cards right," Rick said, "two-to-one these people will show us right where the city is once we get chummy with them. Everyone just follow my lead, and we'll be waist-deep in treasure."

Rose's experience was that whenever she followed Rick's lead, she ended up waist-deep in something, and it was never treasure.

CHAPTER SIXTEEN

Edgar was certain that he'd have been better off staying in England. He'd have been in hospital with a collection of broken bones, but it would have been better than certain death, which he was sure awaited him here in this godforsaken village.

No matter what he'd told Rose, he hadn't wanted to go on this expedition with his father. Nothing about deadly jaguars, tropical insects, and lousy food appealed to him. He'd never understood why his father was so enchanted about these annual research trips that had taken him away from his family and into hellish living conditions. Eventually he'd chalked it up to his father needing an excuse to be away from his son.

But recently, Edgar had gotten himself into a bit of a pickle. He'd been the middle man for a trade of stolen furs for cold hard cash. Prostitutes and an introduction to opium had sent him down a financial sidetrack mid-deal. That led to a shortage of cash to the seller, which led to a shortage of furs to the buyer, which led to both sides wanting to make up their shortages by putting Edgar in hospital for an extended stay.

Edgar found that when you are in the gunsights of two different mobs, friends disappear faster than free beer. With nowhere to hide in all of England, he decided to take the first opportunity to get out of the country. That opportunity was his father's Mexican research trip.

So he'd arrived unannounced, spewing insincere contrition about not taking his father's work seriously, begging to be given the chance to set foot on the golden path to biological enlightenment. His father bought it, and two days later Edgar was on a ship pulling away from a Liverpool dock. He could not have been happier.

And it had been all downhill from there.

Dismal shipboard accommodations, poor weather, awful food. Arrival in Mexico meant new depths to misery as he followed his father through a country that didn't seem far removed from neolithic living. Then they spent weeks in the jungle, an experience that made the worst London slum seem posh. And all of this so his father could collect jaguar poop and measure footprints. Until they'd caught the one in the snare, they hadn't even seen one.

He'd been ready to take the canoe, abandon his father, and paddle back to what passed for civilization. But then these adventurers had arrived and suddenly there was something worth having in this wretched, green hellhole.

Gold.

But as soon as it looked like that dream might come true, boom! He was captured by a tribe from the bloody Stone Age, and he ended up being the only one ready to put up a fight.

As he paced the slaughterhouse hut, he made a promise to himself. With or without these people, and with or without his father, he was going to get out of this damn jungle alive, and with a backpack full of gold. The right opportunity would present itself and then there'd be no stopping him.

***

As the afternoon waned, the entire community began to stir. Through the gaps in the hut walls, Rick could see villagers bustling about, gathering flowers and collecting what looked like torches. Even the children were helping out, carrying items beside their parents. Several women used makeshift brooms to sweep clean a path through the village.

Clarence stepped up beside Rick. "Quite busy out there."

"Something big is going on tonight," Rick said.

"It is the peak of the full moon tonight. Some kind of accompanying ritual is common among many cultures."

"Maybe it's a party in our honor," Rick said.

"Not likely. The torches and decorations I've seen them carrying are very intricately made. These people have been preparing for this event for quite some time."

"There goes my hope that they would treat us like gods," Rick said.

A group of women descended on the pile of their gear outside the hut. They loaded themselves up and carted it all off out of sight. Edgar dashed over from the other side of the hut and slammed a fist against the wall.

"And there goes the rifle," he said. "I told you we should have smashed out of here while the gun was still within reach. Now that, and everything else, is gone."

Rick didn't have a chance to respond to Edgar. A group of men approached the hut. Four warriors with sharp spears accompanied the chief. They stopped outside the hut and one of the guards opened the door. The chief stepped in. He carried a staff topped with the skull of a small jaguar. A long, red cape draped his shoulders. The golden trim along the edges looked like actual spun gold. Rick moved to place himself between the chief and the rest of the group.

The two of them exchanged hard stares. The chief broke eye contact first. Rick knew that was a good sign.

The chief spread his arms and said a few sentences. Rick didn't know what he said, but the tone was welcoming and conciliatory. He waved for Rick to follow him and he stepped out of the hut.

"Oh, hell no," Rose said. "There's no telling what they have planned for us out there."

"Yeah, Rick," Carlos said. "I got this picture of giant pots of boiling water and us being put in them."

"He's inviting us," Rick said, "not forcing us."

"Whatever event is about to go on," Clarence said, "it was already planned before we arrived."

"Remember," Rick said, "we're not prisoners. We're being treated like guests here. Let's not insult the host."

Rick looked to Rose. If she didn't follow, none of them would. She sighed, stepped forward, and looped her arm through his.

"Every time you go to a party without me," she said, "you just embarrass yourself."

Rick led Rose out the door to where the chief waited. The others followed. All six warriors surrounded them and the group headed out. As they did, a crowd of villagers fell in behind them.

"This is like having prison guards around us," Rose said.

"I like to think this is more an honor guard," Rick said.

"I sure hope so," Rose said.

Very quickly, they got to the edge of the village. There they took a trail through the jungle. The bare, compacted earth indicated that the path had been used for a very long time, but the plants along the route bore the bright green wounds of recent cutting. Villagers had trimmed back the foliage in preparation for their passage.

A half-hour into their trek, they passed a stone post about three feet high and four inches on either side. Carvings along the sides included crosses and the phrase *Spiritus Immundus Prohibere*. A shining metal plate capped the top. A glance left and right revealed that more of the markers stretched off into the distance at regular intervals.

The chief passed the markers by, probably having seen them all his life. But Rick slowed down to give the group a chance to get a better look. Prodding from the trailing guards got them moving again.

"Seen anything like that out here before, Clarence?" Rick said.

"Nothing even close," Clarence said.

"The top of those posts looked like silver," Edgar said. "Other metals would have rusted."

"Do you know what was carved into the post?" Rick said to Rose.

"It was Latin," she said. "A rough translation would be an order for any evil or unclean spirits to not go past that post."

"How would Romans get all the way to Mexico?" Rick said.

"They wouldn't. Catholic Spanish priests would have used Latin. That would also account for the cross carved in the post."

"So what were those supposed to be, some kind of supernatural fence to keep unclean spirits out?"

"Depending on where we are going, maybe to keep them in."

"It proves," Clarence said, "that whatever lies up ahead, the Spanish did know about it."

"And kept it off their maps," Rose said. "Just like in the stories about Tezpaluca."

A hundred yards later, they came across mounds of vegetation, like house-sized blooms coming out of the jungle

75

floor. Great strangler figs covered the mounds. As they passed by closer, Rick could see glimpses of chiseled stone blocks between the thick roots.

"Rosie! Those lumps are abandoned Aztec buildings, overgrown by the jungle. I think the chief has led us straight to Tezpaluca."

"The villagers live in huts when they are so close to the sturdy buildings of a city?" Rose said. "Given how overgrown all this is, people rarely come here. There must be a powerful taboo about Tezpaluca."

In moments the path they were on ended at an open space and a clear view of the Mexican sky. The huge structure before them had been completely cleared of all vegetation, or Rick thought, more likely had never been allowed to become overgrown. A set of steps right in front of him led up to what looked like a football field. The open, dirt-covered rectangle was about the same size and stood on a foot-tall base of chiseled stone. Sloped areas faced the field on each side and looked like they were set up for spectators.

At the far end rose a pyramid. Unlike the smooth-sided ones he'd seen in pictures from Egypt, this one had five large, blocky steps that culminated in an apartment-sized final cube at the top. A staircase ran up the center to the peak. A small fire burned in a firepit before the staircase on the pyramid's first level.

At the edge of the field, the chief stepped up onto the raised section and turned to face the crowd that followed them. The guards used their spears to convince Rick and the others they had gone far enough.

Villagers continued to stream in, creating a crowd around Rick and his party. Their guards now faced outward, keeping the five of them from being crushed. The chief began to speak and the crowd hushed. He gesticulated with the skull-tipped staff, whipped his head about so the feathers of the headdress could flutter, and made his voice boom over the natives. Each time his voice paused with an inflection, the people let out a cheer.

"I have no idea what he's saying," Rick whispered to Rose, "but they are sure eating it up."

Rose didn't answer. She was looking at the playing field base that the chief stood on. Then she pointed to the carved blocks that made up the playing field's base. "Rick, look at this."

He knelt to look at them closer. Aztec hieroglyphs covered the face of the stone. But nailed across the center of them was a silver metal strip about an inch wide. Crosses and the same Latin phrase *Spiritus Immundus Prohibere* were engraved in the band, over and over. The band seemed to run all the way to the corners of the platform, but with the crowd pressing in it was hard to tell.

"I'll be damned," he said. "Just like those posts in the jungle."

"I'll bet this band goes all the way around this field and the pyramid attached to it," Rose said.

Rick glanced around. So far, he hadn't attracted the attention of any of the locals. He pulled out his pocket knife, flipped it open, and prepared to pry off some of that silver band for a closer inspection.

As soon as his knife touched the metal, a horrendous shock coursed through his body. He cursed and dropped the blade. The crowd was still mesmerized by the chief, but Rick garnered the attention of the rest of his party.

"What the hell was that?" he said. "Can that thing be electrified?"

"All the way out here in a lost Aztec city?" Clarence said. "Quite impossible."

"Well, that thing shocked me somehow. I recommend you give it plenty of room. Whatever it is, it doesn't want to be touched."

Edgar pressed a finger to the band and showed no reaction. "It doesn't mind being touched, but it doesn't want to be removed."

"Hmm," Clarence said. "Perhaps whatever energy is protecting it had also kept the jungle from consuming this temple as it did the other structures. That would make more sense than imagining these people keeping the whole pyramid clean with Neolithic tools."

The chief ended his speech, turned around, and set out across the field for the pyramid. The guards prodded Rick and the others to follow. The villagers surged into the field behind them. The chief climbed up to the first section of the pyramid. The guards stopped Rick and the others at the base of the step.

"Whatever's about to happen," Carlos said, "we got ourselves front row seats for it."

CHAPTER SEVENTEEN

While the others were enthralled by the spectacle playing out on the field, Rose was much more interested in the hieroglyphs along the structure's base. She recognized several from her readings back in Savannah: Itztli, ruler of Tezpaluca, Tezcatlipoca, the god of the night sky, carvings of combat poses and human sacrifice. This place was exactly the kind of ritual and worship center Aztec cities had been built around. The chief had led them to an undiscovered wonder.

The sun dipped below the tops of the trees and cast a shadow across the temple area, a promise of the darkness soon to come. Two men climbed the steps with two torches each in their hands. They dipped them in the burning firepit and the torches burst into flames. Leaving one standing on either side of the chief, they returned to the crowd with one torch each. Once there, they passed through the crowd touching their torch to unlit torches. Soon two dozen burning torches lit the field. The bearers placed them in holders along the top of the sloped areas. Golden, flickering light illuminated the field.

As darkness fell, the torches and firepit kept the chief lit up like he was in a spotlight. He raised the skull-tipped staff and shouted a few phrases to the crowd. They cheered in response.

"Does anyone have any idea what the bloody hell's going on?" Edgar said.

"The lunar cycle was very important to the Aztecs," Rose said. "This is probably some celebration of that. Maybe an offering to the gods to give a good harvest or bring annual rains."

Then the crowd began a chant, a series of repeated syllables that sounded something like *oh-kan-taka-lay*. The chants bounced between the field's sloped sides and the noise made the air seem denser.

The chief exhorted the crowd from the pyramid, waving his staff and pounding his feet on the stone. His cape fluttered and the gold trim glowed in the firelight. The chief grinned and excitement danced in his eyes. Glistening sweat formed on his forehead.

The people began to stamp their feet in sync with his. The ground trembled from the impacts. The chanting grew louder.

"If this is the kind of party they throw now," Edgar said, "New Year's Eve must be a smashing wingding."

"I'm pretty good at reading a crowd," Rick said, "and I don't like the sensation I'm getting from this one."

Rose had to agree. The frenzy these people were working themselves up to had an insidious tone. The sky above her was dark, but the mood of the crowd was becoming even darker.

The chief raised his staff and shouted an abrupt command. The crowd on the field parted like the Red Sea before Moses and left an open aisle down the center. Three shadowy figures at the far end began to approach the steps. The two on the ends were much taller and broad-shouldered than the slight figure in the center.

Rose used Rick's shoulder for support and rose to the tips of her toes for a better view. She still had a hard time making out any details about the three people. What she could tell was that the two hulks on the outside marched with a solid purpose. The squirming person they held between them was another story.

When the trio was halfway to the steps, what she saw made Rose gasp. Between the men was the girl in the brightly colored top who'd given Rose her hair clasp. She was fighting like hell against the two warriors that held her, but they carried her so that her feet barely touched the ground. Not a muscle on them flexed as the girl tried to writhe free. She was screaming but the chant of the crowd and the pounding of the earth completely drowned her out.

Rose shook Rick's arm. "Rick! In the middle, that's the girl who brought us our food."

Rick squinted. "You're right. Rosie, you read up on all this Aztec stuff. What are they going to do to her?"

"I don't know, but some Aztecs practiced human sacrifice."

"We can't let them do that to that girl," Carlos said.

The warriors marched the girl by. As they did, she caught sight of Rose. She cried out with her eyes locked on Rose's.

The terrified, pleading look on her face translated her local language in no uncertain terms.

The warriors manhandled her up to the chief. The chief made a circle in front of the girl with his skull staff, whirled around and ascended the steps. The warriors dragged the girl up the stairway a few steps behind him.

Rose was all for letting every culture have its own quirks, but whatever this ritual portended for that poor girl, it wasn't right to force her into it. Some things were just wrong in every culture.

"Rick, we can't let them do this," Rose said. "That girl wants no part of this ritual."

Rick set his jaw. "You're right about that."

At the top level of the pyramid, the chief stopped in front of the little blockhouse. There were two stone columns on the platform between the stairs and the blockhouse. The warriors tied each of the girl's wrists to a column then stepped back to the top of the stairs. They, and the chief, faced what looked like a doorway in the little blockhouse.

The girl looked over her shoulder. Tears ran down her face. She cried out.

Within the chanting crowd, one voice shouted out in response to the girl. Rose soon spied the woman who'd come with the girl to their hut. The woman was fighting her way through the crowd with the passion that only a mother could have. She kept screaming the same phrase over and over as she shoved other villagers out of the way. When she reached the base of the pyramid, one of the warriors around Rose's group grabbed her by the poncho and threw her to the ground.

At the sight of her mother's distress, the sacrificial girl wailed even louder. She pulled so hard against her bindings her wrists began to bleed.

The chief and the two guards ignored her, facing the opening in the pyramid as the chief touched the corners with his skull staff.

Rose's heart pounded in her chest. "Rick, we have to do something."

Rick turned to Carlos. "Ready for a fight?"

"Was wondering what you were waiting for," Carlos said.

"Keep these guys busy for me."

The guards around them faced the pyramid, as awe-struck by the ritual as the rest of the group. Carlos grabbed the shoulder of the closest one, spun him around, and delivered a right cross to the man's chin. The warrior dropped his spear and crumpled to the ground.

Rose caught the spear as it fell.

The other guards realized something was wrong and turned to face the group. Carlos grabbed the closest one and threw him into one of the others. Both men slammed into the side of the pyramid. Warriors from the crowd swarmed Carlos.

Rose handed Rick the spear. "Go get that girl."

Rick leapt over the guard's prone body, and bounded up the steps. Warning shouts rose from the crowd as they realized the ceremony was being disrupted. The men at the pyramid summit seemed either too far away to hear, or too consumed in their ritual to comprehend it. The chief was performing some kind of dance before the door.

But as Rick made it halfway up the steps, the warrior who'd led their capture stepped onto the pyramid. He carried that long, curved weapon he'd had in the jungle. He shouted something at Rick.

Rick kept climbing, spear at the ready, straight for the girl. Based on the speed and volume, the ceremony at the summit and the chief's fevered dancing had reached a peak. The girl looked back to see Rick on his way to her rescue. She smiled and shouted with relief.

The warrior set a ball-shaped projectile in the cup of his weapon. Then he leaned back, and with a huge overhead swing, sent the projectile rocketing through the air, straight for Rick.

Rick was just feet from the girl. Then the ball struck him in the shoulder. The impact sent him flat down against the pyramid steps. Rose cringed at the sight. Rick dropped the spear and it clattered down the staircase.

At the pyramid summit, stone ground against stone as a doorway opened in the blockhouse. The chief stepped aside and knelt, as did both warriors. The stink of must and decay rolled out from the opening and down into the crowd. The girl turned back to the doorway and screamed.

A shadowy, hooded figure emerged from the doorway. Tall and thin, it had the shape of a black-cloaked man, but something about its presence said it was most decidedly not a human being. Rose could not make out the face within the hood, but what little light struck it revealed features pallid and drawn.

It did not walk as much as it sailed across the summit to the bound girl. It swirled about her, enveloped her. Her bindings fell away against the posts. The girl passed out.

Then the shadow creature caught the girl and carried her back through the doorway. The stone door slid back into place.

The lead warrior at the pyramid's base called up to the chief, pointing at Rick. The chief and the warriors looked around and finally realized that Rick had come very close to saving the girl.

Rick lay still. From where Rose stood, she could not even tell if he was still breathing.

CHAPTER EIGHTEEN

Itztli held the village girl tight as the stone door closed behind them. The sounds of the chaos on the pyramid steps became a muffled rumble. After centuries of flawless offerings, he had no idea how this one could have gone so wrong.

He stood in a landing at the top of the circular staircase that descended through the center of the pyramid. A series of oil lamps built into the walls lit the interior, one of the more ingenious innovations in the design. Naturally rising oil beneath the building was routed through clay pipes to sconces on the walls. He could see better than a human at night, but even he could not see in total darkness.

The girl squirmed harder. He could let her go. There was no escape with the door closed. But he was not in the mood to hunt her down through the pyramid's myriad passages. Not after tonight's fiasco. He needed her quiet.

He'd worn the black, hooded cape to keep his form as mysterious as possible. He pulled back the hood and then turned the girl around so she could see his face. He smiled.

Her mouth dropped open in abject terror.

He knew what she saw. Pale skin, a nose and ears with tips shriveled into sharp points, red glowing eyes, and of course, his canine teeth longer and sharper than even those of his jaguar servants. A vampire's appearance always struck humans dumb with fear. The effect certainly made hunting them easier.

The girl's eyes rolled up in her head, and she fainted. Itztli sighed in relief as her body went limp. He laid her down on the landing floor. He needed to know what had gone wrong out there.

He closed his eyes and searched for the consciousness of the one who wore the golden jaguar neck collar, the chief, Necalli. When he sensed the familiar thought patterns, he probed the chief's mind, shuffling through the most recent memories. One shocked him.

White intruders?

Since Itztli's imprisonment here, no white men had ventured to Tezpaluca. What would bring them here after so much time? Two had come first, then five more arrived. Necalli was convinced they were emissaries from the gods. The idea made Itztli laugh. These people were not even aware of the gods who ruled the land they had violated. Only now was Necalli regretting his mistaken assessment, and admitting that he should have followed the advice of Ocotlan and had the intruders put to death.

Itztli cut off the psychic connection. The humans would sort this out back in their village. Thanks to their offering, he now had everything he needed within the pyramid walls.

He scooped up the limp girl and carried her down the long, winding flight of stairs. They passed by landings that opened to each level of the pyramid. Despite the shadows within the room, the lamplight still managed to make bright some of the surfaces of the golden treasures within. Back when he'd still freely walked in Tezpaluca under daylight, his people had taken these prizes from other tribes, then used their own wealth against them. Someday soon, he would be able to do that again.

Soon they arrived at a large, circular room in the base level of the pyramid. A mosaic of the moon covered the center third of the floor, encircled by Aztec glyphs that tracked the days and phases of the moon in a perpetual calendar. One corridor led to other now unused rooms. A shelf filled with more plundered gold circled the top of the wall like a halo. Beneath it in the wall were twelve recessed, rectangular, open enclosures. Under each was carved the glyph of their name. His own remained empty, but within the other crypts slumbered the shriveled bodies of the twelve lords who once ruled this realm.

Slumber was not the right word, for his kind never slept, but without feeding, the body became comatose to save energy. His lords had not been awake in centuries, though Itztli had provided drops of peccary blood to their lips to keep them from a lengthy recovery when they finally awakened.

In the center of the room stood a seven-foot-long stone table with the glyph of Itztli carved in the center. Here he'd made the offerings to the god Tezcatlipoca. Now it was where he'd place the offering the villagers had made to him.

He lay the unconscious girl down on the slab and then turned her head sideways to expose her neck. He heard the blood thrum through her artery and saw the measured pulse of it beneath her skin. The temptation to drain her dry was overwhelming. After a year of bitter peccary blood, the sweet taste of human blood would be glorious. But this gift had another, higher purpose.

First, he had to sample the offering. Itztli took her wrist and rotated it so her palm faced upward. He placed it to his mouth and made the slightest puncture with his teeth. Blood seeped from the wound and he lapped it with his tongue. He closed his eyes and savored the taste.

His eyes popped open and he clenched his jaw in rage. In anger he threw down the girl's arm.

She was spoiled. The same defect that ran through the blood of generations of offerings also ran through hers, and even stronger. This inbred village had made a rare, recessive gene dominant. She could bear the offspring of another human with no issue, but she could not sire the vampire-hybrid offspring he sought through her. Both mother and child would die in the attempt. He'd seen it too often.

Frustration and fury exploded within him. He bent over the girl and plunged his teeth deep into her neck. Her hot, coppery blood gushed into his mouth and he shivered in ecstasy. With greedy swallows, he drew every drop from her body and with it, the essences of her life itself. When he was finished, the drained, desiccated corpse on the table looked more like a mummy than a human being.

He reveled in the rejuvenation human blood produced. Physical strength, clarity of thought, and heightened senses all came rushing back the way a resurging river refills an empty reservoir. Again, he saw himself as he should be, the vampire king, ruler of Tezpaluca, Lord of the Night.

The joy of this renewal was soon tamped by the reality of his situation. He was still entombed in the pyramid. The spell that protected the silver band that bound him here could not be broken by any man or vampire. But a dhampir, the child of a human/vampire union, could do it with ease. The Spanish priests casting their spell had not even known dhampirs existed. In the specificity of their spell, they left this loophole for Itztli to exploit.

If only the villagers could offer a female with blood untainted by this anti-vampire virus. It was as if Nature had agreed with the Spanish that if vampires could not be killed, then they must be contained, and she had infected the locals to make certain that occurred for eternity.

A revelation hit Itztli like a bolt of lightning. Among the five intruders was a woman unlike any he'd ever seen, with pale skin and red hair. Whatever land she came from was even farther away from Tezpaluca than the land of the Spanish. So far away in fact, that she could not have the poisoned blood the tribespeople had.

She could bear him a son, and then deliver him from the Hell of living forever in these stone walls. Once free, he would resurrect the others and send his twelve lords across the land to conquer and create the empire he had always deserved.

After centuries of failure, Itztli could finally sense success to be within his grasp.

He just needed to get the redhead into the pyramid.

CHAPTER NINETEEN

Rick tried to push himself, but whatever had pounded him in the back had sent him down pretty hard against the steps. His ribs were bruised, if not broken, and doing a push-up hurt like hell.

The chief pointed down at Rick and shouted an order. The two warriors scrambled down the steps, grabbed Rick under the arms and yanked him to his feet. That hurt worse than trying to get up on his own.

The chief descended the steps and came face-to-face with Rick. His cheeks were flushed, his eyes wide. Spittle flew from his lips and he screamed what had to be obscenities at Rick for disrupting the ceremony. He shook the skull staff inches from Rick's face. One of the guards pressed the point of his spear against Rick's neck.

Just as Rick was certain he was about to have his chips cashed in for him, another voice bellowed behind him. He looked over his shoulder to see the chief's top warrior standing a few steps below. The warrior held the curved weapon Rick assumed had been used to knock him to the ground. To his right and left stood over a half-dozen other warriors. The man wasn't shouting at Rick. He was shouting at the chief.

The chief began to yell back at the lead warrior. The men to either side of Rick released him and spun around with their spears pointed at this new contingent. Rick dropped down to a crouch, hoping that being out of everyone's lines of sight might also put him out of their minds.

The shouting match between the two men became heated. Rick could tell that he was in the middle of a coup, and not just physically. His actions had triggered the lead warrior to question the chief's decision to let these visitors attend, and by extension, the chief's very authority.

The mood of the crowd before the temple appeared non-committal, as if the villagers were waiting to support whoever came out on top. Rick did not think that boded well for the chief.

The warrior said something decidedly disrespectful to the chief. Then he waved his followers forward and they began to climb the steps.

The chief stomped his foot. He pointed his skull staff at each of his guards and then forward, ordering them to his defense.

The two men looked at each other, then at the lead warrior's party. Then they stepped aside to let the rebels pass.

The chief's face fell.

The warriors surged past Rick and grabbed the chief. This turn of events seemed to shock the man so much that he offered no defense, incredulous about what was unfolding.

The lead warrior dashed to the chief's side. He pulled the skull staff from the man's hand and then tore the feathered headdress from his head. The lead warrior donned the headdress, faced the crowd, and raised the staff over his head. He barked a short sentence, and then the crowd roared with approval.

Rick wondered if the chief had harbored any inkling of how weak his grasp on power had been. It didn't seem that anyone in this village would miss the man.

One of the warriors yanked Rick back to his feet. He drew an arrow from his quiver and pressed the arrowhead against Rick's chest. The sharp tip stretched Rick's skin. He remembered Geraldo's painful, poisoned death.

But Rick's concern shifted to Rose's safety. A glance to the pyramid base revealed that the warriors protecting the party on their way here now faced them, looking more like executioners. The entire situation had gone south in a hurry.

The warrior to Rick's side reared back with the arrow, ready to plunge it into Rick's heart.

The new chief shouted at him and the warrior froze. The chief added another order and the warrior lowered the arrow. The new chief did not have a look of compassion or empathy on his face. Instead, the look was sadistic. He must have only spared Rick's life in order to make his death something far worse than a single arrow thrust to a vital organ.

The new chief yanked the jaguar collar from the ex-chief's neck. Then he kicked the old man and sent him down hard onto the stone steps. The ex-chief rose and shuffled down beside Rick. The man hung his head. In the space of seconds, his whole life had turned upside down.

Several warriors marched Rick and the deposed chief back down the stairs. At the pyramid base, they joined Rose and the others. Rose went to his side.

"Are you okay?"

"I won't be doing any pull-ups for a while, but I'll live."

Edgar pointed to the warriors around them. "The jury's still out on that."

Then the warrior group herded them back toward the village. The jubilant mood of the villagers had turned to malice. They wanted somebody to pay for the spoiled ceremony, and Rick had no doubt who those somebodies were.

Once they were back in the hut and the guards had barred the door shut, the ex-chief went to a corner and collapsed onto one of the mats. He buried his face in his hands. Clarence leaned against the table and also looked on the verge of collapse. He closed his eyes and took long, deep breaths. Rick couldn't imagine that the old professor had considered that any of this could have happened to him.

Edgar didn't go to comfort his father. Instead, he turned to Rick with anger in his eyes. "What were you thinking? You've cocked-up everything."

"I couldn't sit back and watch that girl get sacrificed," Rick said.

"Well, she got sacrificed anyway," Edgar said, "And now so will we."

"You were closer to that thing that came out of the pyramid, Rick," Carlos said. "What exactly was it she was sacrificed to?"

"I didn't get the best look, but its face was ghostly pale, the features elongated to look less than human."

Carlos made the sign of the cross and muttered some kind of prayer.

"Whoever or whatever is in the pyramid isn't important," Edgar said. "We're forgetting we just found the lost City of Gold."

"I didn't see any gold anywhere," Rose said.

"There must be some in the ruins somewhere," Edgar said. "After all, that pyramid thing is still wrapped in a band of silver."

"That was no decoration," Rose said. "It had the same engravings as the posts around the city, with some sort of spell cast over it to keep it from being removed."

"Like the lock on a safe," Rick said. "And whatever took that girl is what it's keeping locked away."

"The chief could tell us what's going on," Edgar said. "If he spoke any bloody English."

"The hieroglyphs around the pyramid spoke volumes," Rose said. "That was a temple to Tezcatlipoca, God of the Night, dedicated by Itztli, ruler of this city. There were pictures of him drinking the blood of his vanquished enemies."

"I hope that artwork was just to impress people and not historical."

"Aztecs were brutal," Rose said. "It's documented that their rituals included drinking human blood, if only for the shock effect."

"I think you are all missing what these clues all point to," Clarence said. "And as the scientist among you, it pains me to be the one to draw the conclusion. You have a supernatural creature trapped within the pyramid walls. The pictures on the wall depict the king drinking human blood. They worship the god of darkness and the stories say they ruled the night. Terribly sorry, but this sounds like a classic vampire story to me."

Carlos grumbled some kind of prayer and made the sign of the cross again.

"Vampires aren't real," Rick said.

"That seems true now," Clarence said. "But myth often springs from fact. We cannot discount that at some point vampires were real. Perhaps they were real in Tezpaluca, and perhaps the Spanish contained them here."

"Where I grew up," Carlos said, "vampires are real. My grandfather's generation told many stories of fighting them.

They finally drove them from Cuba using silver weapons. Captured ones were staked to open ground and allowed to burn alive under the sun. And the vampire descriptions match what Rick saw come out of the pyramid."

"You sure they weren't telling campfire stories to scare kids?" Rick said.

"I've seen photographs," Carlos said. "Do you think they would fake pictures just to scare kids? And poor people don't keep silver weapons in the family for generations unless they're worried about a real threat returning. Otherwise, we would have sold them and bought a house."

"If the vampire people of Tezpaluca were repelled by silver," Rose said, "then the ring of silver posts would have kept the vampires contained in the city. I don't think the Spanish would have used that much precious silver if all they were worried about was a myth."

"And once contained, the conquistadors drove them back to the pyramid," Rick said, "and sealed them in with that enhanced silver band."

"Or at least sealed in Itztli," Carlos said, "the king."

"You think that's still Itztli in the pyramid after all this time?"

"Vampires are immortal," Carlos said, "or nearly so if sunlight does not burn them up. What else could live in there for so long, alone, in the dark?"

"Something people might consider the god Tezcatlipoca," Clarence said, "and offer it sacrifices."

"This is all ridiculous," Edgar said.

"Might as well confirm it with the expert," Clarence said, "and ask the chief."

"But he doesn't speak English," Edgar said.

"Mankind communicated for thousands of years before we had English, son."

Clarence took a wooden fork from the table, approached the ex-chief, and sat beside him. The chief looked up. The others gathered around them.

Clarence tapped his own chest. "Clarence. Clarence."

Clarence tapped the ex-chief's chest, offered a quizzical look and put a hand to his ear.

The man nodded in understanding and tapped his own chest. "Necalli. Necalli."

"Necalli," Clarence repeated. "Jolly good start right there."

Clarence smoothed the earth between them and then sketched a picture of the temple. The man's drawing skills were almost as good on dirt as they were on paper.

"Necalli," Clarence said. Then he pointed to the picture. "Tezpaluca?"

The chief's eyes lit up at the word. He nodded and spouted an excited stream of sentences in his own tongue, as if Clarence understood more than that single word.

Clarence drew a small figure at the top of the pyramid, then an arrow from the figure pointing away. Then at the tip of the arrow, he drew a detailed picture of the apparition that had appeared to Rick.

"Tezcatlipoca?" Clarence asked.

The chief shook his head. "Itztli."

The chief took the fork from Clarence's hand and drew on the picture of Itztli. He extended two teeth into pointed fangs.

"Seems our worst fears are confirmed," Clarence said. "Bram Stoker couldn't better describe a vampire."

CHAPTER TWENTY

Ocotlan sat in the chief's chair for the first time that morning. He had stood before it a thousand times, and much preferred the view from this perspective.

But the authority that came with this view also came with responsibility. Though he'd longed to be chief for years, his play for power had been spur of the moment, a reaction to the sacrilege the intruders had committed on the pyramid's steps. He could not admit to the people that he had no plan. He could barely admit it to himself.

Chicahua entered the hut. Ocotlan had hunted and swam in the great river with Chicahua since they were boys. Chicahua had stood beside Ocotlan from the first when he'd rallied warriors to depose Necalli. Ocotlan could not ask for one more loyal.

His friend looked concerned. "The people are uneasy, Ocotlan."

"Chief," he corrected. "I am chief now."

"Of course. I apologize, my Chief. The tribe is anxious."

"Last night, they cheered me as I deposed Necalli."

"It seems they expected his immediate death," Chicahua said, "as well as that of the intruder who violated the temple steps. When dawn came and they were all still alive, some began to say we have traded one weak leader for another."

Ocotlan jumped to his feet. "Who says that? I'll show them strength at the tip of a spear."

"It is a widespread sentiment," Chicahua said, "but shallow. The right action will disperse it."

"That action is obvious," Ocotlan said. "I've already decided that these intruders have to die. If they return to their homeland with stories of the Sacred Place, more intruders would follow. But if they disappear, their people would continue to fear treading on our tribal land."

"And Necalli?"

94

"A deposed chief should not be allowed to live with such shame."

"The only question is how do we kill them?"

"A simple execution will not do," Ocotlan said. "The invaders should have died as soon as we presented them to Necalli. Our capturing the invaders was a victory that harkened back to the ancient times, when the great cities sent warriors against each other and Itztli ruled supreme from Tezpaluca. Perhaps this is the chance to revive the old ways, and add a new chapter to the story of our people."

He also saw this as a way to cement his own story in the people's minds, to create that moment where the whole village saw him as the leader he truly was.

He stood and went to a table by the chair. He placed the chief's headdress on his head and then, for the first time, placed the golden jaguar collar on his neck. It touched the skin of his chest and felt unbelievably warm, which was strange since it was metal and should have been cool to the touch. He took the skull staff of the chief and faced Chicahua.

His friend nodded in respect. "You look every inch the chief of our people."

Ocotlan handed Chicahua his atlatl, still wrapped with the red marker of the tribe's First Warrior. Chicahua looked shocked as he took the atlatl.

"And now you look every inch our tribe's First Warrior. Lead me to the prisoners."

"Yes, Chief," Chicahua said.

He led Ocotlan back to the slaughter hut. Ocotlan needed no guidance, but this was the tradition, that the First Warrior led the chief through the village, signifying his willingness to face any danger before it befell the chief. This, too, would cement their positions in the eyes of the tribe.

And indeed, those eyes were on the two men as they passed through the village. Anticipation hung heavy in the air. The people had yet to resume any work since the ceremony disaster, hoping some kind of justice would be served, and not wanting to be the one to miss such an event. Ocotlan planned to exceed their expectations.

When they arrived at the hut holding the prisoners, the two guards at the door looked relieved, then excited. Apparently they had also been worried about Ocotlan setting things right.

Ocotlan followed Chicahua into the hut. The prisoners surrounded a sitting Necalli. They all stood and turned to face Ocotlan, all but Necalli that is. The defeated man barely looked up. He displayed the drooping expression of one who knew he'd been beaten. The guards outside the hut stepped in behind Ocotlan, either to keep him safe or to eavesdrop on the chief's remarks. Either reason was fine with Ocotlan.

"You have come and violated our Sacred Place," Ocotlan said to the group. "As it has always been, the punishment for intruders is death."

The tribesmen around him smiled. The captives may not have understood him, but the warriors did, and they were clearly pleased that the intruders' sacrilege was not going unpunished.

"Necalli," Ocotlan continued, "you have disgraced our people and risked the anger of Itztli. I warned you about the intruders, but you were spineless. The punishment for your weakness will be joining these people in death."

Necalli did not even look up.

"We will celebrate their deaths as our forefathers did," Ocotlan said, "on the Court of the Moon."

"Performing the Act of Commemoration?" Chicahua said.

"Of course," Ocotlan said.

Chicahua grinned. "Even in my father's lifetime, we have never performed the Act of Commemoration on the Court of the Moon."

"Even in your father's lifetime, our people haven't vanquished an enemy as completely as we did these intruders, nor saved the villagers and the Sacred Place from their pollution. The old ways are the only way to celebrate that."

The announcement of the Act of Commemoration at the Court of the Moon seemed to excite the guards as well, who looked upon the captives the way wading birds look at small fish.

"Send the women who are supposed to forage today up to clear and prepare the Court," Ocotlan said. "Tonight will be momentous."

Chicahua nodded and departed to execute the chief's orders. Ocotlan headed back to his hut as the guards began an excited conversation about the night ahead. He knew that in short order the whole tribe would know. By night's end, he'd stand over the corpses of the six prisoners, his position as chief would never be questioned, and his name would be glorified for generations.

CHAPTER TWENTY-ONE

Humphrey sat in the open doorway of the flying boat. He gave the handle on the manual bilge pump another few pumps. A slug of grimy water coughed out of the end of the tube and into the river.

The tar patch over the leak was still holding. Mostly. Or it might have been another leak in the twenty-plus-year-old plane. Or it might have been condensation. He sure wasn't going down into the bilge again to solve the mystery. Whatever the cause, Humphrey had to pump the bilge every few hours to keep it dry. As long as he could keep up with the water until everyone got back with the gold, he wasn't going to worry about it. Much.

He was a little concerned that no one had come back yet: not to check on him, not to pick up any more supplies. He supposed that could be a good sign, that they'd found the Lost City of Gold and were slogging back with a thousand pounds of treasure in tow. But it could also mean something had gone very wrong. In retrospect, he wished they'd agreed on one of them stopping by for a visit every day or so.

A splash sounded along the hull. Humphrey leaned over and peered into the water.

The damn fish that had scratched the paint off the hull were back. From the amount of churning water, there were more of them this time, and bigger ones flashed among the school. Tiny, tan particles popped up in the water.

He stomped his foot against the hull and hollered for the fish to take a powder. This time, the school wasn't intimidated.

"Why, you sorry little sons of…"

Humphrey went back into the plane. He grabbed one of the spare oars in the mechanical room and returned to the side of the hull. If the little sons of guns weren't going to leave when asked politely, he'd have to act like a barroom bouncer.

He stood over the most active part of the school and took a golf-type swing at the fish through the water alongside the hull. His follow through left the dripping oar suspended over his left shoulder.

Instead of the water calming as the school scattered, the turbulence increased and fins broke the surface as the fish thrashed harder. It seemed that all he'd done was make them sore.

Humphrey grimaced. "Well, you ain't seen nothing yet."

He jabbed the oar into the water and moved like he was sweeping a floor as he tried to brush the pesky fish off the hull. The water began to froth as the fish got angrier.

Suddenly the oar felt twice as heavy. Humphrey stopped stirring. The oar jerked back and forth in his hand. It felt like one of the fish had grabbed it, and it didn't feel like it was one of the small ones.

Humphrey pulled the oar out of the water. Moving a shovelful of coal would have been easier. When the paddle broke the surface, Humphrey's heart skipped a beat.

A three-foot-long fish hung from the oar. Sunlight sparkled on its silver scales and it had a sleek body like a barracuda. Solid black eyes stared at Humphrey like he owed the fish money. Its gills flared and the fish emitted a hiss.

Humphrey had faced down German Fokkers with steely resolve. But this enormous, spooky fish was entirely terrifying. In a panic, he swung the oar back around toward the nose of the plane in an attempt to dislodge the fish. The pesky creature hung on tight.

With the extra weight at the end, Humphrey couldn't stop the swing. He came all the way around and the oar slammed into the side of the plane over the open doorway.

Then the fish let go and disappeared into the cabin.

"Hell's bells!"

Humphrey rushed into the plane. The fish lay on the deck next to one of the passenger chairs. It flopped back and forth, slapping the wood. Its gills flapped open and closed as its mouth yawned in search of oxygen it could process.

A solid view of that mouth gave Humphrey a whole new cause for alarm. The fish's jaws were lined with broad, sharp teeth. He'd seen open bear traps that looked more inviting. He had no doubt that thing could take off a finger or maybe a hand if he got too close to it, which he had no intention of doing.

In a few moments, the fish stopped moving and its malevolent, black eyes turned glazed. In an instant, a rank, algae-tinged stench filled the cabin. The space would be unlivable unless Humphrey got that thing back in the river.

Dead or not, he sure as heck wasn't going to touch it. He pointed the oar down to sweep the creature back out the door.

Then he noticed the edge of the paddle. The fish hadn't bitten down on it, it had eaten it. Big chunks of the edge of the paddle were missing. He thought back to the bits of wood he'd seen in the water when the fish dispersed before.

These damn termite fish weren't scraping off the paint. They were eating his wooden veneer airplane. And if they chewed a hole in the hull, he could flail at the pump like a madman but he wouldn't keep this plane afloat.

He flipped the deceased termite fish out the door and it hit the water with a splash. He hoped the dead fish would give the rest of the school pause. He was disappointed. The fish took the death of their compatriot in stride, and the water along the hull continued to churn.

It was going to take more than a stomp on the deck or a swipe with an oar to get rid of these pests. Humphrey smiled.

"Let's see how y'all like the soothing tones of a Liberty engine."

Humphrey figured that between the propwash, the roar, and the vibration of the hull, firing up one of the engines ought to scare the hell out of them.

He scrambled up into the cockpit and took a seat. He threw some switches, adjusted the fuel mixture, and hit the starter for the left engine. The little motor whined as it labored to turn the big V-12 Liberty. The engine belched a cloud of black smoke and then roared to life. Humphrey adjusted the throttle to rev as much as possible without overcoming the current. No point driving upriver dragging the anchor.

With the engine warmed up and stable, he decided to savor his victory. He looked down over the side.

The fish hadn't missed a beat. He wondered if he took off, would they be clinging to the hull like the one on his paddle?

This was a serious problem. He didn't have a lot of extra gas to burn if they expected to make it back to Cuba, and stopping for gas with a plane full of gold in Mexico was an only marginally better idea than having Pinocchio go for a river swim here. He couldn't believe that the shock of the engine running hadn't scattered the school.

Shock. That was it!

The big Liberty was putting out some serious voltage recharging the onboard batteries, with plenty left over for all the aircraft systems. The fish might stand the noise, but there's no way they could handle electrical current.

There were clamps and cables and extra guide wires onboard. He just might be able to turn the river into one big electric chair.

He killed the engine and got to work.

***

Thirty minutes, and a lot of fish-induced hull damage later, Humphrey finished wiring up what he hoped would be the fishes' doom. From the main power connection in the mechanical room, he'd used clamps and guide wires and a spare switch to get positive and negative electrodes into the water along the hull. When he threw the switch, electricity would arc through the water and zap the fish. The wooden hull would be an insulator and keep him safe. He hoped.

Actually, most of his plan was based on hope and a bunch of suppositions that this Aeromarine 75 ran like his Ford Tri-motor. But this was the only plan he could come up with.

He zipped up to the cockpit. A look over the side confirmed the fish were still hard at work, and there was a good chance there were more of them. Seemed that word had spread that the Aeromarine buffet was open for business.

Humphrey fired up the engine and backed it down to idle.

He climbed down to the electrical connection in the mechanical room under the cockpit. On the way he looked over at the fish churning up the water. The school stretched from the stern to the bow.

"We're about to have ourselves a fish boil."

Humphrey entered the tiny space. The thrum of the engine seemed to be amplified within the walls. He eyed the old throw switch he'd used for this half-assed project. It was kind of rusty, but rust was iron and iron conducted electricity, so rust could only make the connections stronger, or at least that was what he thought to himself.

But he really didn't have time to overthink this plan. Every second he wasted meant there was that much less hull underneath his feet. He took a deep breath, grabbed the switch, and threw it.

The panel exploded in a shower of sparks. A rush of electricity blasted through his body and slammed him against the wall. He saw stars and slid down to the deck.

When his senses returned, the quiet told him the engine had stopped. That was bad. Not only had he electrocuted himself, he'd electrocuted one of the two engines this big flying boat needed to takeoff. It wouldn't matter if he'd saved the plane from the termite fish if it only had one working engine.

He remembered the termite fish and wondered if they'd gotten hit even half as bad as he had.

Wobbly legs and screwy equilibrium convinced him to settle for crawling to the cabin door. He did and then stuck his head out the opening.

Dead fish floated all alongside the hull. There were so many that if he could have walked across them, he could have almost made it to shore. A number of them were several feet long.

"Glad y'all got a taste of that medicine. Hate to have kept all that fun to myself."

But now he had a whole new problem. One of the Liberties wasn't any more useful than the anchor off the bow at this point. When the group returned to an unflyable plane, they'd be furious. Carlos would have murder in his eye for sure. Humphrey vowed that as soon as he could stand on his feet again, he was going to take off some cowlings and see what kind of damage he'd done.

But that moment wasn't quite at hand. He lay on the deck and sighed.

At the edge of the mat of fish corpses, several moved and caught Humphrey's attention. He looked over just as the biggest, blackest catfish he'd ever seen surfaced. It had a mouth three feet wide and when it opened, two dead termite fish were sucked inside. Then the catfish submerged.

"There ain't a damn thing in this river that ain't dangerous."

Then a few yards from the plane, something nudged a patch of floating carcasses from underneath. It made a torpedo-straight line for the flying boat. Humphrey gripped the doorway opening.

A splash at the side of the hull sent several fish sliding over their deceased neighbors. Then came a sound Humphrey thought he'd never have to hear again. A termite fish began to gnaw at the hull. It was as if it had been waiting for the crowd of fish to make room for it.

"Next time," Humphrey said, "I'm letting Carlos stay with the plane."

CHAPTER TWENTY-TWO

As the chief and his warriors left the prisoners in the hut, Rick exhaled in relief. He'd feared they were all about to die when the armed men crowded in. Instead, the chief had said his piece and left them unscathed. For now.

Rick gave the door a push, on the off chance that the guards had not relocked it. It did not move.

"Sure wish we had a translator for that speech," Carlos said.

"Necalli's reaction translated it quite perfectly," Clarence said. "We're in a tight spot."

"That's an understatement," Rose said. "If we were only in a tight spot, we'd already have been killed. The fact that we haven't been means there's something worse than a simple execution planned for us."

"Do I want to ask what?" Rick said.

"We can start with the human sacrifice I mentioned earlier," Rose said.

"I don't fancy being fed to that Itztli thing out there," Edgar said.

"And it could get worse," Rose said. "Traditional Aztec treatment of prisoners was brutal."

"We could still smash out of here," Edgar said. "Make a run for it."

"The guards outnumber us and the villagers look like they want us dead," Rick said. "An escape in broad daylight isn't a bet I'd make. If we're going to try that, we'll wait until dark when we have some advantages."

"I hope the spiders and jaguars aren't hungry tonight," Rose said.

***

As dusk fell, no one had delivered any food or water to the tent. Rick took this as a bad sign that the tribe wasn't wasting food on ones who were about to die. No one came to check on the former chief. His lack of supporters was another bad sign. A loyalist external rescue wasn't in the works.

Suddenly, outside the hut, the whole village seemed to stir to life at once. It was as active as when they'd prepared for the sacrifice last night, but this mood was more fiery than festive. A number of villagers passed by the hut and peered into the gaps between the sticks, eyes filled with malice.

Rose sat beside Rick on the ground. She nudged him. "I know that look on your face. You are thinking the same thing I am. We're out of luck."

Rick was embarrassed he'd let his face betray his concerns. His mantra was to fake it until he figured it out, and that attitude had always gotten them through.

"We're never out of luck. I once pulled a straight flush with a four-card draw holding nothing but a three of hearts. We just need to keep in the game."

Rick stood and addressed the rest of the group. "We need to get out of here before that new chief does whatever it was he promised to do when he was in here. We'll make a break for it in a few hours once these guards start looking sleepy. Carlos, Edgar, and I will rush the door and break it down."

Rose pointed to Necalli, who sat in a corner with his eyes closed. "We're taking him with us, right? They're going to kill him because he was decent to us."

"Absolutely," Rick said. "I think we can get him to understand we're escaping. The rest of you see if you can *quietly* take that table apart and we'll use the legs as weapons."

The other men went to the table and turned it upside down. Necalli gave them a quizzical look, then sighed as if he'd given up on any hope of escape. Rick stepped over to the firepit and began to tear the front pocket liners out of his pants.

"What are you up to?" Rose said.

"Applying some science. Watch the master at work."

He knelt down and began to grind up charcoal between two of the large stones that ringed the firepit. Rose joined in. When they had a few ounces made, Rick swept them into the cotton cloth pocket with his finger.

"Now we need to seal this up," Rick said.

Rose picked a long thread free from the top of the bag with her fingernails. She handed it to Rick.

Rick made the pocket as puffy as possible, and then used the string to tie it shut.

"What are you going to do with that?"

Rick smiled. "Once we start our escape—"

The door burst open and a squad of spear-carrying warriors swarmed into the hut. Necalli stood, dusted the dirt from his skin, and faced the men with his chin raised. That was the look of a man ready to face death with dignity. Rick preferred to not meet death at all.

Then the new chief entered carrying the skull staff. He wore the headdress, wristlets, and neckpiece Necalli had worn at the pyramid ceremony. Necalli eyed him with seething anger. The new chief stood before the former and made a pronouncement that sounded uncomfortably like a prison warden reading a prisoner a death sentence. Necalli looked him straight in the eye. When the chief turned and left, Necalli followed him out the door.

"Maybe they stopped being interested in us," Rick whispered to Rose.

As if in response, several warriors began to prod the captives out the door after Necalli.

"Looks like they still are," Rose said.

"Here's a time I'd like to be less popular," Rick said.

"Time for you to draw that straight flush," Rose said.

CHAPTER TWENTY-THREE

Other guards carrying torches had been standing outside the hut. They fell in ahead and behind the warriors and their prisoners. The guards walked Rick and the others through the village. Despite all the earlier activity, now there wasn't a soul to be seen and the village was dead quiet save for the tramp of the party's feet.

"This is spooky as all hell," Edgar said. "If I'd shot the buggers straight off, none of this would have happened."

Darkness fell and the torchbearers' light created a yellow glow over the group, a moving illuminated island in the deepening night. Rick recognized the familiar path the new chief took. "He's taking us back to Tezpaluca. Rosie, is that good news or bad news?"

"At this point, I think that all we have coming is bad news," Rose said.

This time when they arrived at the ruined city, no people lined the way to the playing field as they had before. Instead of the raucous noise of that crowd, only the chirp and buzz of jungle insects broke the silence. They arrived at the steps to the playing field and the temple beyond. The new chief led them up the steps and stopped the group at the edge of the field. The space had been cleared of the encroaching jungle flora, and the stone surface scraped clean.

The chief turned and raised his skull staff in the air. He made another announcement, then gave an order to the torchbearers on the right and left of the group.

The two men sprinted up the field. The flames of the torches trailed behind them like they were carrying comets. Unlit torches stood set up in a row along the field's two sides. As the torchbearers passed, they made the flames from their torches lick the heads of the others and set them ablaze. They stopped at the base of the pyramid and lit the firepit on the steps. The glow joined that of over a dozen burning torches along each side, bathing the playing field in light.

The missing villagers sat in the sloped viewing areas, shoulder to shoulder, facing the field. At the lighting of the last torch, they rose to their feet and cheered. The sound echoed within the field and reminded Rick of what a lion's roar had to feel like to the trainer in the cage with it.

The chief marched downfield, up the pyramid steps, and to the other side of the crackling firepit. The light shining up on him sent chilling dark shadows across his face. He continued to exhort the crowd while the guards pushed Rick and the group down to the equivalent of the thirty-yard line.

Clarence grabbed Necalli by the shoulders. "Necalli, what is going on?" He added a bunch of questioning hand signals and facial expressions.

Necalli answered with some violent-looking hand motions including striking his palm with his fist and striking his forearms together.

"That's a lousy answer," Carlos said.

Just then, a group of women with laden arms approached them. The guards let them pass. The women dumped their burdens in a pile, then began to pick up items one at a time and fit them to Rick and the others. In a few moments, each of them wore a vest made from a thatch of palm leaves with a yellow circle in the center and a helmet made of a half-coconut shell.

One woman offered Necalli a headdress similar to the one that his usurper now wore. But it was smaller and, unlike that multi-colored version, this one was made entirely of yellow parrot feathers. He refused to take the headdress. One of the guards prodded him with a spear. Necalli reluctantly took the headdress. He put it on his head and then his shoulders slumped.

The women retreated to the sidelines and two others rushed out. One had a cup of liquid in her hands, the other a collection of spears. The one with the spears handed them out to everyone in the group. Rick checked the spearpoint on his. It was fashioned out of tree bark.

The second woman went person to person and smeared a stripe of yellow paint under each person's eyes. Rick's first inclination was to wipe it off, but he assumed that that would just earn him a second application at the tip of a spear, or worse.

"Surrounded by this crowd," Clarence said as he examined his faux spear, "I feel uncomfortably like a gladiator."

"You aren't far off," Rose said. "These are all stylized armor and weapons. We're about to be part of a combat reenactment."

"What's that?" Edgar said.

"The Aztec celebrations often included reenactments of famous victories as a way to get the people to feel patriotic."

"Two-to-one we aren't playing the good guys," Rick said.

Up on the pyramid, the chief donned a mask that resembled one of the faces carved in the pyramid walls.

"See," Rose said, "the chief is wearing the face of Tezcatlipoca, assuming the role of the god whose favor made the victory possible."

"And casting himself in the role helps cement his role as the new leader, no doubt," Clarence said. "No wonder Necalli is so mad."

The chief raised the skull staff over his head and the crowd cheered. The warriors who surrounded Rick and the others retreated and formed a line along the end of the court behind them.

"It appears that our participation is mandatory," Carlos said.

The chief pointed his staff at Rick's group. The crowd hissed like a den of irritated snakes.

"Yes," Rick said, "we're definitely not the hometown favorites."

"The only ways off this field are through the people in the stands or past the warriors at the edge of the field." Panic permeated Edgar's voice. "There's no way out."

"Rosie, you said it's a reenactment." Rick smacked the tree bark tip of his spear against the ground. It broke. "No one's going to get hurt with these toy weapons. When the supposedly good guys arrive, we'll pretend there's combat, we'll pretend to die, and see what rewards our good acting brings."

The chief raised his staff overhead and shouted a command. From both corners of the pyramid beside him came a dozen warriors. Their face paint had multiple colors, as did the feathers at their shoulders. They all wore heavy, leather vests and what Rick thought looked like leather football helmets. They carried spears, and one carried one of those strange curved devices one of the warriors had used in the jungle. The warriors lined up along the far end of the field. An archer rose into the stands on each side.

"Their armor looks a lot more protective than ours," Carlos said.

"And I don't want to be the one to say it," Rick said, "but it looks to me like those weapons are tipped with real stone points."

"This won't be a reenactment," Edgar said. "It's going to be a massacre."

CHAPTER TWENTY-FOUR

At the appearance of the warriors in full battle regalia, the villagers went crazy, cheering and jumping up and down. The crowd was not rooting for the underdog.

This deck was stacked against Rick's party. If Rick had been taking bets on this game, he'd have put the odds of the visiting team winning at 1000-to-1.

"Back-to-back, everyone," Rick said. "We need to hold them off, knock them down, and get some real weapons."

Everyone backed up. Rose's shoulder touched his on his left. Clarence stood inches away on his right.

"These things only end one way," Rose said. "They kill us all."

"We've been in worse situations than this."

"When was that?" Rose said.

"Just stay close," Rick said. "No one's getting past me to get to you."

The warriors split into two squads that headed in opposite directions around the group. Each squad spread out, then did a multi-step dance as they formed two counter-rotating circles. All the while they did this, the chief shouted to the crowd. The villagers responded with cheers.

As the warriors circled, one raised his spear, then dashed toward Edgar. Edgar held his spear across his chest with both hands, ready to try and deflect the jab.

But the warrior stopped short of the group, made several mock thrusts at Edgar, and then rejoined the swirl of men.

"They're going to drag this out," Carlos said.

"They aim to give the crowd its money's worth," Edgar said.

Then Necalli shouted some kind of a war cry. With his pseudo-spear slashing through the air, he rushed at the circle of warriors.

"What's he doing?" Rose said.

"Showing everyone he's still a chief." Rick realized that if the man could disrupt the circle, that might make a hole the group could rush through.

An archer atop the stands to the left let fly an arrow. It whizzed through the air and struck Necalli through the yellow circle on his chest. The arrowhead punched through the man's back with a spray of blood. The impact spun him around, then he dropped to the ground and did not move.

The crowd cheered. The circling warriors did not miss a step.

"We're not getting out of here alive." Edgar turned to Clarence. "I can't believe I'm going to die on one of your damn field trips."

With Rose's life at stake, Rick wasn't about to give up. He noted that all the warriors, like the rest of the villagers, were much shorter than even Rose. "We have the reach on them. Poke them in the eye before they get close enough to stab you."

"And if they throw the spear instead?" Rose said.

"Plan on ducking."

The warriors began to move faster around the group, accelerating to a run. Individuals made more frequent feints at increasingly closer distances. One made a jab at Rose. Rick stepped forward and with an upward sweep of his spear sent the warrior's spear up in the air and the warrior tumbling backward.

Nearby members of the audience laughed. The warrior's face reddened and fury burned in his eyes. He rejoined the group.

Another warrior came straight at Clarence. The old man wobbled as he tried to gauge where the warrior was going to thrust his spear. He judged wrong. Clarence lunged forward with his spear, but the warrior had already danced sideways. Then he brought his spear down in a slashing motion. The point ripped across Clarence's exposed shoulder and down his arm. The professor screamed and fell to one knee.

The warrior's focus had remained on his victim too long. Rick flipped his spear around and caught the warrior unaware with a hard thrust to the side of the head. The man's head snapped sideways and he dropped his weapon. He fell to the ground and crawled back to the warrior circle.

Rick scooped up the spear. He tossed his faux one to Rose, who caught it with her right hand. She made a defensive X across her body with her two shafts.

Clarence rose. His spear shook in his right hand. His left arm hung limp at his side. Blood ran from his shoulder and a red stain grew down the back of his shirt.

"Are you okay?" Rick said.

"I…I can't move my fingers." Clarence looked over his shoulder but had no good angle to see the wound. "Is it bad?"

"I've seen worse," Rick lied.

The warrior's fall at Rick's hand seemed to break the ceremony's spell on the other warriors. They stopped circling and eyed the group, and especially Rick, with vengeance.

"I don't think we were supposed to fight back," Carlos said.

The warriors charged the group.

One came straight for Rose with his spear pointed at her heart. As the point passed over the top of the X she'd made with the spears, she pressed her hands together. The intersection of the X slid up over her head and took the point of the spear with it.

The shocked warrior could not stop. When he was right in front of Rose, she drove a knee up between his legs. His leather armor might have covered his chest, but this tender spot remained exposed. The warrior cried out, dropped to the ground, and curled into the fetal position.

Carlos was not so lucky. Three warriors converged on him, far more than he could handle. He managed to send one reeling with a spear strike to the side of the head, but the swing left him exposed. The other two drove their spears through his palm frond armor and took him down to the ground.

Two others pounced on Rick. One came at a run and just feet away, launched his spear.

Rick twisted sideways to let the spear sail by, then charged the now unarmed warrior. He ran his spear into the man's chest. The warrior staggered sideways and collided with the other attacker. Both ended up on the ground.

Rick grabbed the spear dropped by the man Rose had incapacitated. He turned to see that their cause was doomed. There were too many warriors. Clarence was down on his knees, swiping his tree-bark spear between two attackers. Edgar and Rose were fending off warriors hand-to-hand. And in the background, villagers surged out of the stands in their direction. It looked like everyone wanted a piece of this action.

Rick decided if he was going to die, he was going to do it at Rose's side. He dashed toward her just as another warrior closed on Rose with a stone-point knife raised high.

A screeching cry from the chief at the pyramid froze every villager in position. All faces turned to the pyramid. Rick turned as well, but it wasn't the chief that caught his eye.

At the pyramid's peak stood the black-hooded figure from the night before. Itztli carried the body of the sacrificed girl in his arms. Her limbs hung limp in the way only the dead can endure.

Itztli heaved the girl's corpse into the air. It dropped down onto the pyramid steps, then bounced and cartwheeled all the way to the bottom where it stopped near the feet of the chief. The chief lowered his god mask to look at the body.

Itztli pointed a long, white finger at the chief. "Your offering is rejected!"

Rick was taken aback. First, Itztli spoke in English. Second, Rick hadn't actually heard it. The voice had echoed inside his head.

The crowd gasped. Apparently, they could hear Itztli as well as he had, and understood him. The chief went to his knees and raised his hands in submission.

Itztli swiveled and pointed his bony finger at Rose. "Bring me her instead and avoid my wrath over this insult."

Rick's jaw dropped. *How could Itztli know who Rose was or even that she was here?*

Rose screamed. Rick spun about to defend her. But several warriors had converged on her and now surrounded her like a wall.

"Rose!" Rick took one step toward her and then something hit his head with a crack. He went dizzy and fell to his knees. Another one of the balls that had downed him last night rolled by him on the ground.

A blinding headache and a wave of nausea conspired to keep him down. Rose shrieked again and that cleared his head in a flash. He stood and forced his eyes into focus at the pyramid. The chief led a group of warriors up to Itztli. They carried a writhing Rose over their heads.

"No!" Rick ran for the pyramid steps and made it to the fire burning at the base.

He was too late. They'd already carried Rose to the peak. The warriors set her before Itztli. She tried to run, but Itztli grabbed her by the throat and squeezed. He lifted her up and she beat her fists against his face. Then she choked and passed out. Itztli threw her over his shoulder and carried her back into the pyramid.

Rick felt his heart break. His Rose was gone in the hands of some awful creature, a creature that had just killed the last woman to enter the pyramid.

The shock of Itztli's return had dampened the mood and the bloodlust of the crowd. Mesmerized by the events at the pyramid's peak, no one intervened as Clarence and Edgar ran up beside Rick.

"Rick, I'm so terribly sorry," Clarence said.

"I'll get her out of there." Rick said it with an amazing amount of certainty for a man with no clue how to do so.

The chief and his warriors noticed Rick and the others near the firepit at the base of the pyramid. As if remembering they still had people to kill, they came running down the steps. The crowd on the field seemed to have the same realization and began to surge in Rick's direction.

"We need a miracle," Clarence said.

Rick remembered the pouch in his pocket. "Better; we have science. Get down and cover your ears."

He took out the pouch, gave it a very violent shaking, and threw it in the firepit. He ducked and pressed his palms over his ears.

The firepit exploded. Even thunder sounded tame compared to this blast. The boom made the ground tremble. Chunks of burning wood flew from the pit like a shotgun blast and landed all over the pyramid and field. Embers burned skin and villagers screamed. At this flash and bang, likely brighter and louder than anything any of them had ever heard, the villagers seemed dazed and scared.

Rick spied a gap between the corner of the pyramid and the seating along one side of the field. The crowd didn't block the way. It might be their only hope for getting off this field alive.

Rick pointed to the opening and shouted to Clarence and Edgar. "Follow me!"

CHAPTER TWENTY-FIVE

A smack to the side of the head awakened Rose.

She opened her eyes, remembered what had just happened to her: the shock of Itztli singling her out in the crowd, the terror of being swept up the pyramid by a mob of men, the panic of having the life choked out of her in Itztli's cold, iron grip. Her pulse began to race.

She hung head-down over Itztli's shoulder. He was descending steps inside the pyramid and she bounced with each drop. The throbbing on the side of her head hinted that a bump against these stone walls was what had awakened her.

Itztli clamped her ankles with both hands and it felt like she'd been shackled in steel. No matter how much she struggled, breaking free wasn't a possibility. For now, she opted to fake still being unconscious.

The steps hugged the walls of a circular, central shaft in the pyramid. Lamps built into the wall gave enough dusky light to make out most details. The surface contained hieroglyphs all along the staircase. She recognized a few that referred to Tezcatlipoca and there were some pictures of gruesome battle scenes. None of them made her feel less scared as Itztli made his way down.

The stairway ended in a large, circular room. Overhead, a crystal orb glowed as if it had electric lights within it, but Rose knew that was impossible.

Along the top of the wall, a wide shelf ringed the room, filled with a fortune in gold objects. There were platters and goblets and Aztec artifacts made of the precious metal.

Below the gold-laden shelf, the walls contained twelve rectangular recesses three feet wide and two feet high. In the gloomy interior of each, Rose swore she could make out the top of a human head and was reminded of mausoleum walls filled with vaults of the dead. Under each opening was one of twelve hieroglyphs, and Rose thought of the twelve lords that ruled under Itztli long ago.

A stone table that looked like an altar sat in the center of the room over a mosaic of the moon and circled by Aztec glyphs. The glyph of Itztli was carved into the center of the table. Drops of what looked like dried blood speckled the surface. Itztli dropped her down on the altar and she couldn't help but moan on impact.

"You're awake."

Rose sat straight up. Itztli stood beside the altar. His hood lay back on his shoulders and exposed a hideous face, drawn, pale, and pointed. A pair of fangs extended out over his lower lip. She struggled not to scream, not to betray how terrified the sight made her feel.

Just as outside the pyramid, she'd heard his voice in clear English, though was also certain that Itztli had made no sound. She rolled off the other side of the altar and then dashed for the far wall.

"I'm not going to hurt you," Itztli said. "But I can't have you running around the pyramid unsupervised."

Faster than what was humanly possible, Itztli was at her side. He grabbed her around the waist and swept her across the room with such speed she felt like she was flying. He dropped her down beside a shackle attached to a long, iron chain. An eyelet sunk into the floor secured the chain's other end. He clamped the leg iron around her ankle, stuck an iron bar through the lock holes in it, and then in a feat no human could match, he bent the rod into a U and effectively locked the shackle closed.

"That should hold you," Itztli said. "It's held all the others."

Rose wondered how many other women had been shackled here over centuries, with none ever escaping.

Of course, none of them had Rick working on their rescue.

With her initial shock receding, Rose evaluated her situation. Even if she was certain she could open the door at the pyramid's peak, she couldn't outrun Itztli up all those flights of stairs. A shadowy corridor on the far side of the room went somewhere, but she doubted that it was going to host an exit door to the pyramid's base. She was going to have to think her way out of here, and she needed more information from Itztli to hatch a plan. That meant she needed to choke back any fear and get him talking. "You won't hurt me the same way you didn't hurt that poor girl you dumped down the pyramid steps?"

"If I wanted you dead, you already would be. I need you very much alive."

"These people think you are Itztli, the last ruler of Tezpaluca."

"That's because I am."

"That can't be," Rose said. "Itztli had to have died six hundred years ago."

"And yet I did not. Tezpaluca was once a great city, looked upon with favor by the God of the Night Sky. So great was our devotion that Tezcatlipoca gave the ruling families the gift of immortality."

"By your appearance, at the cost of your humanity."

"Like trading swampland for a mountain peak," Itztli said. "We were gifted with enhanced strength, keener senses, plus the telepathy that lets me read some minds and communicate with all without speaking. And we sustained ourselves on something more satisfying than the sad fare you humans consume."

Itztli waved something forward from the darkened corridor behind him. A black jaguar trotted out, carrying a limp peccary in its mouth. Like an obedient dog, it dropped the mammal in Itztli's outstretched hand, then sat back on its haunches.

Itztli raised the creature to his lips. His canine teeth extended and then he bit into the peccary's neck. The creature shuddered as Itztli swallowed gulp after gulp of the animal's blood. As he did, the creature shriveled and its fur turned gray. Rose remembered a similar look to the poor teen's corpse that Itztli had dropped outside the pyramid.

Itztli threw the shrunken carcass to the floor. The jaguar retrieved it and then trotted back into the corridor. Hope that there was indeed an exit there swelled in Rose's chest. Then she heard the grinding of stone against stone and was certain that whatever passage the cat had used had closed up after it.

Itztli looked at her and smiled with bloodstained teeth.

"Then you are a vampire," Rose said.

"That was what the Spanish called us."

Rose needed to probe him for a weakness. "So as the legends say, the villagers' sacrifice to you had to be at night, because you can't tolerate daylight."

"We best serve the God of the Night Sky under that sky. Better to rule in darkness than to serve in sunlight."

Rose summoned the courage to sound dismissive. "You call yourself a ruler but for centuries you've stayed hidden inside your crumbling mausoleum."

"Trapped, not hidden." Frustration filled Itztli's voice. "The Spanish came for Tezpaluca last. They slaughtered the humans who served us, then drove us back into the heart of the city. We are immortal, but we can be wounded, though almost all wounds will heal. In a final battle, we killed the Spanish by the dozens, but one by one we fell, until I was the last to succumb with three swords in my chest. The other lords and I awakened in the depths of the pyramid and soon found we could not leave. Spanish priests had wrapped the base in enchanted silver, a barrier we could not pass and we could not remove."

Rose recalled Rick being shocked touching the blessed band around the wall. "And neither can the villagers."

"The priest's curse said no man or vampire could ever break the spell."

Rose laughed. "So like a pet, the villagers deliver you human sacrifices to feed on?"

Itztli's eyes narrowed. "Hardly. The jaguars bring enough prey to barely sustain me as the rest of my lords in the walls of this room lie sleeping. The villagers' offering serves a greater purpose than food, but one for which this last offering, as all the previous offerings, was unfit. That would be to bear my child."

The idea of young women being delivered to this monstrosity to be some kind of forced bride made Rose both disgusted and furious. "Why would you even want that if the jaguars can barely sustain you?"

"Because while neither man nor vampire can break the spell confining me here, a dhampir, the hybrid of both is neither. My son will walk down the steps one night, destroy the cursed band, and set me free. Then I will feast and grow strong again, then bring back human prey to rejuvenate my people. Once awakened, we will reclaim our lands and our destiny to rule the world."

"No woman would let you do that to her."

"Her acquiescence would not be required. But no matter, because so far, none were fit for the task. The villagers somehow have tainted blood and are unable to accept my seed."

Rose wondered if Nature had set in motion a natural defense against this threat so close to them and had sparked that evolutionary change.

Itztli sprouted a malicious grin. "Then you and your un-poisoned blood arrived."

Rose's skin crawled. "I will never consent."

"Again, acquiescence is not required. When you are fertile, we will mate. The jaguars will bring in food to keep you alive until my son is born. And his first meal will be to feast on your blood."

CHAPTER TWENTY-SIX

Standing beside the pyramid firepit, Rick knew his parlor trick explosion was going to buy the group a few moments of time. He sprinted for the gap between the stands and the pyramid corner. Clarence and Edgar were right behind him, but not in that order. Clarence's wound had taken a toll. He supported his dead left arm with his right hand and he winced in pain each time a foot hit the ground.

Rick reached the corner and it was clear why the designers had left this gap. A long spillway angled down to the ground in the gap. Those monsoon rains had to get off the playing field somehow. Slick, wet slime covered the flat surface. It was a good fifty feet down to the ground.

From behind them came a chorus of shouts and commands. The chief ranted about something from the pyramid steps. Feet pounded the field and Rick knew they were about out of time.

"They're coming!" Edgar shouted.

Rick jumped for the spillway and landed on his butt. The steep, slippery surface offered no resistance. Rick rocketed down the spillway. Once below the level of the field, the torchlight vanished, and the moonlight was all that lit the scene. Even if he could have seen where he was going, he had no control. He bounced and turned and skidded. Every flex and stretch he made to try and stabilize his slide only seemed to make it worse. He skidded left and his arm grazed the pyramid wall. His shirt tore and it felt like his skin caught fire.

He jerked hard back to the right, so hard that he rolled onto his stomach. He dug hands and toes into the spillway, but there was no purchase against the slimy surface. He was heading heels first to whatever awaited him on the ground, with no idea how imminent that impact was.

Then he looked up to see the soles of Edgar's boots a mere yard from his face. The man wasn't having any better luck managing his descent. Once Rick stopped at the bottom, two hundred pounds of Edgar would land on his head, break his neck, and kill him.

Or, assuming Clarence was on his way as well, the professor would crush them both.

He thought fast, then reached up and grabbed Edgar's ankles. Then he either pulled Edgar to him, or pulled himself up beside Edgar. He couldn't tell which and did not care. Edgar tried to push him away, but with one more yank Rick pulled himself even with Edgar and wrapped his arms around the man's chest.

Tree branches whipped past them and Rick knew they were close to the end. "Bend your knees!" he shouted in Edgar's ear.

They both did so just as they hit the bottom. Rick yanked Edgar sideways and the two of them rolled across the ground. Rick let Edgar go and they ended up side by side in the dirt.

Then Clarence screamed.

The moonlight provided enough light that Rick could make out Clarence lying on the ground at the base of the spillway. Rick scrambled back over to the old man. Clarence moaned.

"Clarence, how bad is it?"

"My ankle…it's probably broken. And my head struck something on the way down."

Rick felt so sorry for the man, a professor so far out of his element. "We need to get away from here. Those villagers will come looking for us. We'll get you up and moving."

Edgar joined him. His eyes narrowed. "Bloody hell. You're a mess."

Up atop the playing field, a number of villagers shouted and waved torches in the air. Rick doubted they could see the three of them so far away, but they'd still assume they were down here.

"Edgar, get to his other side." Rick realized Clarence wasn't going to go far in his condition. "We need to hide."

The two of them lifted Clarence. He moaned and passed out.

"That's either a good thing to save him the pain," Rick said, "or a bad thing if he has a concussion."

The two carried Clarence down the overgrown remains of the Tezpaluca street. Rick thought it best to stay in sight of the pyramid. Rose was in there and he wanted to be able to get back to her. They came to the remains of a small stone building. Half of it had collapsed and it had an open doorway.

"In here," Rick said.

The room in what still stood of the building was just under ten feet on each side. Dirt covered the floor and roots grew down through cracks in the ceiling. The damp air reeked of decay. He'd bet that the last person to set foot in here had been an Aztec.

They set Clarence down in a corner. Rick checked the old man's pulse. It was steady, but weak.

"We need to get farther away," Edgar said. "They'll be back around looking for us."

"We can't risk moving your father until we have some daylight to check his injuries." Rick examined the room. "It doesn't look like anyone but us has been here in centuries. The rest of this city may be taboo. But it won't hurt to cover the opening a bit."

The two of them went to work and in a short period of time had covered the threshold with a combination of fallen stone blocks and uprooted plants. The camouflage wouldn't hold up in the daylight, but it would work well enough in dim torchlight.

They sat down beside Clarence in the now very dark room. Edgar sighed.

"My father should never have come out here," he said. "He's too old to be chasing jaguars through the damn jungle, and way too old to be running from homicidal natives."

"We'll get him home," Rick said, "along with Rose."

"Say, what was it you threw in that firepit?"

"That bag was full of charcoal dust," Rick explained. "When I was a kid, I was stupid enough to sweep up a pan full from the floor around our fireplace and then throw it into the fire instead of outside like my mother told me to. The dust exploded, singed my shirt, earned me a spanking, and taught me that charcoal dust was combustible. I gave the bag a few shakes to get the dust floating around inside, then when the cotton caught fire, the dust inside exploded."

"A cloth hand grenade," Edgar said.

"With much more sound than force," Rick said. "But a good distraction for people who've never seen that kind of flash and bang."

"You wouldn't happen to have a few more of those with you, would you?"

"I only had time to make that one. We're going to have to rely on darkness and silence as our defense for now, and hope that the whole village doesn't start combing through the city ruins looking for us."

***

Ocotlan stared down the spillway at the darkness blanketing the city ruins. Chicahua stood beside him with a torch in one hand. Behind them stood the murmuring mass of the villagers. The chief seethed with frustration. With every warrior in the village at the ceremony, it was inconceivable that the intruders had escaped. The celebration that was supposed to cement him as the chief had humiliated him instead.

"Assemble half the warriors," Ocotlan said. "I want the intruders brought before me, dead or alive."

"Now?" Chicahua said.

Chicahua would never have questioned Necalli's orders. His response made Ocotlan even more angry. "Yes, First Warrior. Before they get too far away."

"Chief," Chicahua said, "the moon is setting soon. Our torches burn low. The warriors have been up since sunrise and have been exhausted performing the ceremony."

"The warriors, and you, will do as I order."

"Itztli's jaguars rule the night. Tezpaluca is forbidden outside the Court of the Moon. Those are the laws."

Chicahua was right. Ocotlan risked further angering Itztli. He was likely already furious about the chaos that erupted at the reenactment, even more so at whatever magic the intruder had used to unleash the power of a thundercloud at the pyramid steps. The ritual tonight had likely weakened Ocotlan's hold on power. A display of Itztli's displeasure would break it completely.

Ocotlan took another look to the base of the spillway. "The intruders likely died in that fall. Their broken bodies probably lie right there. Lead everyone back to the village. At daybreak take a hunting party back here. Return with the intruders' corpses, from wherever you have to find them."

Chicahua nodded. Then he went back to the crowd and began to relay Ocotlan's commands.

Ocotlan reassured himself that Itztli could still be well-pleased. He had to be. Even with the unravelling of the Act of Commemoration on the Court of the Moon, Ocotlan had done the most important things Itztli had commanded.

He'd delivered the female with hair like fire.

CHAPTER TWENTY-SEVEN

As sunlight began to force the night into remission, Rick wondered how much sleep he'd gotten. It sure didn't feel like much. Between being on alert for warriors searching the ruins and worrying about what was happening to Rose, real rest had been impossible. Each time exhaustion forced him unconscious, apprehension jumped in and thrust him back wide awake. The advent of dawn was his excuse to stop trying to sleep.

With the increasing light, he could get a better look at their accommodations. The building looked like it had been twice as large to start with, but the collapsed roof acted like an angled wall across the center. Moss-covered hieroglyphs covered the walls. Rose could have read some of them and Rick added another item to his list of reasons he wanted her back beside him.

Edgar lay snoring beside one wall. Clarence still sat up in the exact same position they'd placed him last night. Rick had a bad feeling that the old man had died. Rick crawled over and checked his pulse. Still throbbing. Clarence was one tough old bird.

Rick crawled back to the doorway and looked out over the blocks they'd piled to partially fill it. He'd made a good choice in stopping here. The pyramid was just twenty yards away across an open space.

Edgar crawled up beside him. Rick thought it odd he hadn't checked on his father first.

"We made it through the night," Edgar said.

Rick was about to respond when leaves rustled over to the left. His first thought was of the village warriors. With daylight's arrival, the chief might send them after the three escapees. Rick shushed Edgar with a finger to his own lips and ducked down. A glance around the room revealed no useful weapons left behind by the previous occupants several hundred years ago. He grabbed a fist-sized stone from the ground and got ready to bean someone with it. With Rose held captive, he wasn't going down without a fight.

Rick raised his head enough that he could just see over the top stone block. Edgar peered around the other corner. Rick wondered how many warriors the chief would send to capture the three of them. Humiliated by their escape, the chief would probably send them all.

Leaves rustled again to the left. Rick tensed.

A black jaguar emerged. It carried a peccary in its mouth. It stopped in the shadows and stared straight at the two men in the ruins. Then the big cat slunk away.

It took an indirect route, keeping to the ruins' deepest shadows, and zigzagged over to the pyramid. At the wall, it paused before an opening just a bit larger than itself. It dropped the peccary in the gap, pushed it forward with its nose, then crawled in behind it and disappeared.

"Where am I?" Clarence rasped.

Edgar left the doorway and went to his side. "We're hiding in the city ruins next to the pyramid. As soon as it's full light, we're pushing on out of here."

Clarence shifted his position and moaned. "I think I'm too broken for that, son."

"And I was nearly killed last night. Damn brilliant this whole expedition idea was. And now we're hiding outside a jaguar's den."

Clarence's eyes fully opened. "A den?"

"Sure. We just watched one take a peccary through a hole and into the pyramid."

"Jaguars sleep in trees," Clarence said, in the bored tone of a teacher repeating a fact for the hundredth time to a dense student. "Not dens."

Motion at the corner of his eye drew Rick's attention back outside. A second jaguar emerged, this one carrying a guanabana. It took the same convoluted route to the pyramid wall. A few yards short of the wall, the fruit slipped from the creature's mouth. It rolled away into a patch of sunlight.

The jaguar approached the fruit in a slinking crouch, like it was hunting it. It paused, as if mulling over what looked to Rick like a pretty simple problem to solve. The jaguar glanced back at the opening just as the first jaguar reemerged. The first cat trotted back through the shadowed route, past the second cat without acknowledgment.

As it came to the closest point to Rick's hiding place, the returning jaguar's eyes again locked on Rick's. With its previous prey tucked away, Rick was certain it was about to add a human or two to its stash. But instead, the cat hurried back into the undergrowth and disappeared.

The second cat uttered a frustrated growl as it sat outside the patch of sunlight. Then it swiped at the guanabana with one paw. The fruit rolled into the shade.

But as soon as the cat's paw had come out of the shadows, it had begun to sizzle. It was as if the jaguar was under a broiler, not sunlight. The jaguar uttered a noise somewhere between a hiss and a roar and yanked its paw back into the shadows. Smoke rose from its fur. The jaguar furiously licked its paw until the steam stopped rising.

Then the creature hobbled over to the guanabana and put it back in its mouth. The cat hugged the shadows even more closely, made its way to the pyramid opening, and crawled inside.

Rick went over to Clarence. The old man looked terrible, with skin so gray he could pass for a corpse. He glanced at Clarence's ankle. The man's foot faced at an angle so awkward it made Rick wince. He looked back at Clarence's face and hoped he hadn't betrayed his reaction.

"You needed that sleep," Rick said. "We'll get you back to the plane and straight to a city with a hospital."

Clarence waved away Rick's promise as a transparent lie. "The jaguar. You saw it take a peccary into the pyramid?"

"Yes. And a second one just brought in a guanabana."

"That's abnormal behavior. The jaguar would eat such small prey right away. It's bringing the prey to Itztli inside the pyramid. That's the fresh blood he needs to survive."

"A trained jaguar?"

"Or thought controlled. Itztli spoke to all of us telepathically. He could be able to command lesser creatures."

Rick thought that would explain the jaguar skipping the opportunity to attack the three of them when they'd be fish-in-a-barrel inside this ruined building. The big cat already had a mission from its master.

"So, it was bringing the peccary for Itztli," Rick said, "and he only needs blood to survive. The guanabana, which the second jaguar was unfamiliar with carrying, would have been to keep someone else alive. And the only someone that could be would be Rose."

"That's a reasonable conclusion."

Rick was ecstatic to have a little evidence, however indirect, that Rose was still alive in the pyramid.

"Something else," Rick said. "The jaguars went out of their way to travel in the shadows."

"A natural feline behavior."

"But when it stuck a paw in bright daylight, it was like the fur caught fire."

"You saw flames or smoke?"

"Well, smoke, I guess."

Clarence started to cough. His hacking got so violent he bounced back and forth against the wall. A trickle of blood dripped from the corner of his lips and he wiped it away with his good hand.

"The jaguar we caught in the trap looked like it had all the moisture in its body cooked out of it from the inside. It didn't make sense that it could become so desiccated in just a few hours. It must have happened when the rising sun hit it in my snare, just like it started to happen when the jaguar's paw was caught in the light."

"So whatever supernatural force turned Itztli and his people into vampires," Edgar said, "created vampire jaguars?"

"It would sound crazy if we hadn't seen all we've seen the last few days."

"It certainly explains why the jaguars are so strictly nocturnal," Clarence said.

"And having to care for Rose as well has forced them to work past dawn," Rick said. "This is good information. Now we have another weapon—"

Clarence began to cough again. But this time it was more like choking. He spit up gobs of bright red blood. When he paused, he looked at Edgar with watery eyes. "We discovered something amazing, didn't we?"

Edgar was staring out the opening and didn't even turn around.

Clarence fell back against the wall. His head rolled to one side. A burbled rattle wheezed out through his lips and his whole body sagged in surrender to death.

A wave of sadness washed over Rick. The professor didn't deserve to die just because he wanted to research jaguars.

Edgar turned around and stood, his face contorted in anger. "And there you have it. I told him not to take this damned trip, and he did anyway. And now he's dead."

"He did discover something he thought was pretty amazing. He seemed to think his sacrifice was worth it."

"Well, he wasn't the only one sacrificing. This cocked-up holiday also got me stuck in vampire-infested ruins in Mexico. I knew I should have stayed home."

Rick knew Edgar didn't mean what he was saying. All the stress they'd been under plus his father's death added up to more than anyone should have to endure.

"Look," Edgar continued, "let's get out of here before the chief sends his goons in after us. We'll head straight for your plane, takeoff, and never think about this place again."

"No dice. I'm not leaving without Rose."

"You have to be realistic. How long do you think he'll keep her alive in there? And even if you find her alive, who knows what the bastard's done to her. Quite likely you won't want her back."

Rick's blood boiled. He slammed Edgar against the wall and grabbed his shirt at the collar. He twisted it until Edgar choked.

"She's alive," Rick said. "And I'll always want her back."

Edgar gasped and raised his hands in surrender. Rick released him. Edgar gulped air like a landed fish.

"Fair enough," he gasped. "What's your plan to get into that pyramid?"

Rick looked over at the structure. "Same way those jaguars did. Right through that opening."

CHAPTER TWENTY-EIGHT

Once there was enough daylight to safely travel, Rick led Edgar out of their hiding place and back to the outskirts of Tezpaluca.

"We should be going straight for the aeroplane," Edgar said. "They'll be out here hunting us."

Rick had kept a sharp eye and open ears for any warriors that might be scouring the jungle for them. He hadn't seen or heard a thing. "If they were, they would have found us long ago. There're no signs we're being pursued."

"Maybe that's because they move like the wind. Recall how they surrounded us and we didn't hear a thing?"

Rick had to admit Edgar was right about that. But entertaining that kind of paranoia would paralyze them. "If they're looking for us, the further we move from the lost city, the less likely they'll find us."

Rick had made Edgar bring two grapefruit-sized chunks of stone from the rubble of their hiding place. He carried two himself. Edgar lifted the rocks he held in his hands. "If they find us, you can't very well expect us to fend them off with these."

"We didn't bring these to defend ourselves. You'll see why we have them soon."

As they walked the jungle, Rick hunted around for one of the silver-tipped posts that ringed the city. At last, he found one and brought Edgar to it.

"Silver is Itztli's weakness," Rick said. "The vampire legends talk about it, everything we've seen around this city confirms it. If these markers kept the vampires from leaving the city, they ought to keep Itztli off our backs. I'm going to guess that silver might even hurt him, the way steel can hurt humans."

"Marvelous, let's bet our lives on your guesses." Edgar kicked the base of the stone pole. "Expecting we'll just pluck this out of the ground and carry it back to the pyramid, then?"

"Nope. That's what we brought the rocks for."

Rick adjusted his grip on one of his stones so the pointier end stuck out from the bottom of his fist. He took aim at the post just below its silver tip.

"Hold up," Edgar said. "You're going to bash that silver bit free? Remember what happened when you tried to take off the silver band around the pyramid?"

He hadn't thought about that. Rick checked the inscriptions on the pole. "I don't think this has the same protective inscriptions on it that the silver band had."

"You can read that Latin?"

"No but I can tell it's different than the band had."

"That might be a question of grammar, or a few words cut out to save some space."

Rick was already committed to the plan. "If it's protected, you can say 'I told you so.'"

Rick reared back and brought the stone down hard. The impact sent a little shockwave all the way up to his shoulder. What it didn't do was blast him like the pyramid band had. It also sent a spray of dust and stone chips into the air.

"These chunks of carved stone block are much tougher than this centuries old Spanish concrete," he said. "All we need to do is beat a bunch of these silver tips free. Start working your way around the ring and let's take up a collection."

Edgar gave Rick a reluctant look, but turned and headed in search of the next marker. Rick lost sight of him in the plant life, but soon heard the muffled sound of stone cracking against stone.

He went back to work on his own pole and soon had the silver tip broken free from the base. A few smacks between two rocks pulverized the concrete inside the tip and it sifted out like hourglass sand. What he had left was an inscribed silver cone about three inches long and two inches wide.

He wasn't sure how many of these he'd need to take on Itztli and save Rose, but he was willing to go for overkill. He set out in search of the next marker in the ring.

***

About an hour later, Rick returned to where they had started. He'd had one brush with a band of warriors, but he'd been able to hide and they'd passed by without seeing him. The close call reinforced that he had to get Rose out of the pyramid soon. He couldn't avoid being discovered out here forever.

Edgar was already at the initial marker, waiting for Rick. Rick wondered how long the man had been waiting. He would not have put it past Edgar to bring back an excuse instead of any silver tips.

"How did you do?" Rick asked.

Edgar held out three silver tips in one hand. "That's it. I couldn't find another post after these."

Rick doubted that. He'd had no problem finding posts and seven sat in his pockets. Of course, several centuries was a long time and the jungle was unforgiving.

"I don't know how protective an ounce or two of silver is going to be," Edgar said.

"These were enough to keep the vampires contained in Tezpaluca. They at least made vampires sick. I don't need to kill Itztli. I just need him out of commission long enough to get Rose out of that pyramid."

Edgar put his three pieces in his shirt pocket. "So this is my magic shield, then? I'd certainly fancy a magic weapon instead."

"That's a better idea. Something good for defense and offense at the same time. A silver-tipped arrow would be great."

"I'm sure if we went back to the village," Edgar said, "they'd be happy to loan us a few so's we can go kill their vampire god."

Rick ignored the sarcasm. "There's not much out here that we have the time or skill to fashion into a weapon." Rick remembered something he'd seen in a suit of medieval armor Rose kept him from buying. "Unless we're the weapons."

Rick set his stones on the ground and then hunted up a stick about as big around as his finger. He took one silver cap and put it over the stick. Then he went back and knelt by the stones. Using one stone as a makeshift anvil, Rick picked up the other and began to hammer at the malleable silver. In a short period of time, he had the silver pounded into a lumpy fit around the stick. He pulled out the stick about a half inch and then beat the tip flat.

"That's the world's worst arrowhead," Edgar said.

"That's because it isn't an arrowhead." Rick pulled the stick free, and then slipped the silver tube over his index finger. It covered the digit nearly up to the knuckle. He rotated it until the flat edge was vertical. "It's a claw."

"You'll have to get much closer to Itztli than I'd prefer in order to use that."

"If that's what it takes to get Rose back, that's what it takes. I'll make three more of these. An armored silver hand might be enough to have Itztli keep his distance. Then we'll go save my wife."

CHAPTER TWENTY-NINE

Rose awakened from dozing against the wall. For a brief moment, she was unaware of where she was. As the realization came to her that she was Itztli's captive in the bowels of his pyramid, anger and frustration set in.

She'd banished her fear hours ago. That had been her first reaction after being forced down here. But she'd assessed the situation and knew that being afraid, letting dread become her master, would only incapacitate her. Being physically manhandled by the warriors and delivered here was something she couldn't have resisted. But being psychologically manhandled by Itztli was something else. She was a mental match for any man she'd ever met. She bet that applied to vampires as well.

Itztli was nowhere to be seen. It was a large pyramid, and she had no idea how many rooms and corridors it had, or what Itztli did to pass an eternity of captivity here. She really didn't want to know.

The recesses in the walls around her were filled with more vampires, all tucked back into the shadows. Eleven more blood-sucking monsters lay ready to awaken and devour the human race. Even though they were dormant, or whatever their state of vampire existence was, Rose's skin crawled from being so close to them.

She knew not to give up hope, and that was because she knew her husband. Rick wasn't going to abandon her to captivity here. He'd come up with a plan. It might be an outlandish, high-risk, impulsive plan, but he'd come up with one. And then like a dog with a bone, he wouldn't let go of it until he executed it. All Rose had to do was be ready to help him when he did.

Of course, being chained to the floor was going to make being helpful pretty difficult. She checked the shackle around her ankle. Itztli might have easily bent the iron pin that held it closed, but there was no way she could. Opening the clasp wasn't going to be her ticket to freedom.

She pushed aside the guanabana the jaguar had delivered for her. Then link by link, she inspected the whole ten-foot section of rust-pocked chain. It was worse for the wear from centuries of use, but still seemed strong enough to hold an elephant in place, let alone a human. She realized that she was likely doing what every prisoner shackled here had done across all those decades, looking for a way to get free of this chain. The disheartening reality was that none had ever succeeded.

She worked her way back to the iron eyelet anchored in the stone floor. It had been driven down into the stone and then packed all around with mortar. The Aztecs weren't big mortar users, or iron for that matter. They preferred to cut stones for a perfect fit so no mortar was needed. The mortar and the chain it held in place were all borrowed Spanish technology.

Based on every old building she'd ever seen, mortar did not last forever.

She sat down, braced herself against the wall, and set a heel against the eyelet. She cocked her leg and gave the eyelet a hard kick. She swore her knee absorbed all the impact. After a deep breath or two, she tried again. The results didn't seem much better. Brute force, or at least the level of brute force she could deliver, wouldn't break this thing free. She crawled over to give it a closer look. Tiny grains of mortar ringed the base of the eyelet. Rose grabbed it with both hands and twisted.

It moved.

She instantly dismissed her observation as the fruit of wishful thinking. She tried to twist it in the other direction.

It did move! She caught herself before she shouted that aloud.

Not much, just a fraction of a fraction of an inch, but it moved. What force couldn't dislodge, physics would. With enough back-and-forth twisting, she could grind the mortar around the eyelet into powder, and then out the eyelet would come. Once she got it free, she might be able to make a dash up the steps and out the door at the pyramid peak, if she could figure out how to open it.

She imagined the look on Rick's face when he arrived to rescue her and she was waiting for him in Tezpaluca.

Footsteps sounded on the stairway above her.

Rose shifted her position so she blocked the view of the eyelet from where Itztli would be standing in the room. With her hands behind her, she might even be able to keep working the eyelet while he was there.

Itztli descended the stairs and went straight to the altar in the room's center. Then as if on cue, a jaguar emerged from the corridor across from her. Rose thought that of course it was on cue, since Itztli controlled the jaguars telepathically. It was like he'd called for a servant.

The jaguar carried a peccary in its mouth. The cat trotted over to the altar, put its front paws on the top, and dropped its master's offering between them. Then it loped back to the corridor and waited on its haunches.

Itztli grabbed the peccary and chomped down on its neck. As he took greedy swallows from the creature, the poor peccary shriveled in the vampire's hands. When he'd finished, he tossed the carcass and it landed at the feet of the waiting jaguar. The big cat picked up the carcass, and vanished down the corridor.

If she could telepathically talk with that jaguar, she'd make it a hell of a deal to leave that exit open for her so she could crawl out with it, even if it would have been a very tight fit.

Itztli had ignored her since their first conversation. She had felt him probe at her mind, though. That had been very different from hearing him speak to her telepathically, which had been like listening to him speak through a loudspeaker, a detached, impersonal, one-way conversation. But having him probe her mind was like a stranger reaching a hand up her dress, an exceptionally invasive and unwanted event. She'd done the mental equivalent of slapping his hand, and after the second try, he stopped.

Rose wasn't going to allow Itztli to roam around in her mind, but she did need to get him talking. He'd have to reveal more about himself if she was going to find a weak spot to exploit.

Itztli looked over at her and at the guanabana that she hadn't eaten.

"You need to eat that before I make you eat it."

"I refuse."

"Humans have two purposes, to toil as servants or to become food. Choose not to be the first, and you can surely become the second."

"Then you will have no son," Rose said.

"I can feed without killing you. I'll drain you to a point of weakness, let you recover, and do it all again."

Rose liked the idea of being helpless in front of Itztli even less than being killed. She could not believe how callous he was. "Do you forget that you used to be human?"

"You were once an infant. Do you look back on that era when you were helpless and ignorant as a golden age of your pathetic existence? Tezcatlipoca has elevated me to a reality far superior to anything humans can experience."

"So you think you're a god, like he is?"

"No, but I'm closer to a god than you are to a vampire." He pointed to the glowing orb above. "The beams of the Mooncaster are Tezcatlipoca's gift, a reminder of the joy and energy the moonlight brings. I will again walk freely under that orb soon enough."

"*You* will?" Rose made a circling motion pointing to the recesses in the wall. "Or *all of you* will?"

"All will. In time. Immortality means I have time to avoid mistakes. All may rise, but only those who are loyal shall stay risen. The strongest and the bravest are the ones destined to rule the world."

Itztli had let something slip. It sounded like the Mooncaster did more than light the room, that it delivered some kind of life force as well. Perhaps that is what sustained the comatose vampires in the walls, while the blood sacrifices were the extra energy that kept Itztli from falling into that same deep sleep. After all, even claiming to be immortal, no creature could sleep for several hundred years without some form of energy.

Rose also gleaned something else from the conversation. Itztli may have had a powerful grasp on the poor villagers, but that authority did not automatically extend to the other vampires in this room. He planned a staged awakening, and likely no awakening to any he thought harbored some disloyalty. What kind of power struggle had preceded the group being bound inside this pyramid? Whatever it was, the sleeping vampires would think it had happened yesterday when they woke up.

Rose wasn't sure how she could use this information to her advantage. She pondered the options as she reached behind her and continued the minute movements of the eyelet that she hoped would be the key to her freedom.

CHAPTER THIRTY

As soon as Chicahua was certain there was enough daylight to reclaim the jungle from the jaguars, he had sent several warriors to scout the area around the Sacred Place. Now he led a warrior band back to the pyramid itself in search of the escaped intruders. They marched back to the Court of the Moon.

His men were wary. The city was forbidden to enter, and setting foot on the court was only allowed during the prescribed rituals. He didn't share their concern about incurring the wrath of Tezcatlipoca. He only paid lip-service to the silly religious notions because it was required of a warrior, more so now as First Warrior. He did not believe that some all-powerful god controlled their world. And while a strange creature they called Itztli did live within the pyramid walls, Chicahua didn't know why the villagers had to serve it. The girl Itztli had cast down the steps of the pyramid had been his cousin. What purpose had her death served? What had Itztli given in return?

He was only concerned with returning to the village carrying the intruders' corpses, proof that they would not return to their land and bring even more trespassers back with them.

At the Court of the Moon, Chicahua bounded up the steps and went straight for the corner spillway, the last place he'd seen the intruders. His men followed with tentative steps, as if the ground might open at any moment and swallow them up. At the top of the spillway, Chicahua looked down to the bottom.

Ocotlan had said no one could have survived the drop. He was wrong. There were no bodies lying on the ground. The intruders were still alive.

Chicahua cursed. Now he would have to find them. And the first place to search would be the city ruins, starting at the spillway's base where the intruders had started.

"Follow me," he said to the others.

The central spillway surface was slick with algae and moss, but the raised edge was not. Balancing along it, he began the steep descent. Half-way down, he looked back up at his warriors. They all still stood at the top, looking scared.

"Get down here!" he ordered.

"But the city is forbidden," one answered. "Tezcatlipoca will strike us dead if we do."

"I will strike you dead if you don't," Chicahua said.

He made it to the bottom and jumped to the ground. He barked another order to the cowering warriors at the top. They gave each other fearful looks, then one-by-one followed their leader down the spillway's side. As they descended, Chicahua inspected the area around the spillway. There were many footprints, a lot of churned earth, and drops of blood. The drop hadn't killed the intruders, but at least one of them had been injured. That meant they might still be close.

The warriors made it to the bottom. They looked quite relieved to have not been struck dead. Chicahua shook his head. This was another example of how foolish notions confused his people.

He ordered his men to search the ruins. They began to, but never out of line of sight with their leader, still anxious about what supernatural punishment their trespass might bring.

Chicahua noticed a lot of stones with new scrape marks beside one collapsed house near the pyramid's side. He went over and stuck his head inside.

One of the intruders lay dead in a corner. It was the old one, the one who wore the crystal coverings over his eyes. Blood soaked the side of his body and his ankle was badly broken. Chicahua called over the other warriors and they all entered the building.

"Look, this intruder is dead. Not killed by Tezcatlipoca, but by a warrior's attack on the Court of the Moon. The others could not save him, and they ran. They will be long gone. We will return to the village."

The warriors left the building, clearly happy that they were heading home without a god having brought fire from the sky down upon them.

Chicahua reached down and took the crystal covers from the intruder's face. He placed them over his own eyes. Everything around him suddenly looked sharper and brighter. He removed the covers and the world went back to normal.

This was more proof of what Chicahua had observed. These intruders came from someplace with technology created by nothing less than magic: metal blades that cut and did not dull, clothing woven tight from fine thread, and shoes and belts made of strange animal skins. Now there was this device that sees the world in a whole new, magnified way.

He stepped back out of the building and looked at the pyramid with disgust. Generations of worship here had done nothing for his village, while people from other lands had discovered many amazing things. Perhaps the time had come to go in a new direction, a time for change.

Ocotlan wasn't yet secure in his leadership. There would be no better time for Chicahua to assert his own in its place.

CHAPTER THIRTY-ONE

Several hours later
The trip back to the pyramid was tense. Rick was on the lookout for any more roving warriors as well as any dangerous wildlife. The balance between moving quickly to save Rose and treading softly enough to stay hidden was difficult to maintain.

Edgar also worried the hell out of him. He hadn't warmed to the man during their time together, and in fact probably trusted him less now than before. Edgar didn't mourn his father's death, he definitely didn't prioritize rescuing Rose, and Rick was certain that he'd cut and run if Rick mentioned the option of heading for the plane right now. Rick had encountered Edgar's self-centered type at many a gambling table. They always walked away losers. Rick promised himself to hedge any bets the two of them shared.

The two came to the edge of Tezpaluca. The pyramid loomed in the distance down the main road. Rose was still breathing somewhere in there. Rick could practically feel it. She'd fight tooth and nail to stay alive. He'd do the same to get her out.

The sound of feet tramping on the path came from behind them. Rick and Edgar scooted sideways and ducked behind a pile of overgrown ruins.

A group of eight warriors appeared. The chief in full ceremonial regalia led four others carrying spears and arrows. In the center of the group marched a prisoner with his hands bound behind him. The two warriors that trailed the group carried what looked like stone posts over their shoulders.

As they came closer, Rick could tell that the chief leading the group was not the same man who had deposed the first chief, the one who'd captured them in the jungle. This was a new, younger man, but he wore all the trappings of the chief, save for the gold jaguar neckpiece. The warrior who had captured them in the jungle was the man imprisoned. The jaguar neckpiece still hung from his neck.

"Looks like the village is under new management," Rick said. "Again."

"Can't say I'll shed a tear over the chap who tried to kill us," Edgar said.

Unlike the last deposed chief who stood proud in captivity, this new one hung his head, dejected and depressed. It seemed that his rapid rise and swift fall were more than he could bear.

The group marched down the main street to the playing field and the pyramid beyond.

Rick nursed a newly sprouted hope. "Maybe they are going to trade him for Rose."

"I don't think they want her back as much as you do," Edgar said.

"Probably true. But if they offer him to Itztli, we might be able to get the jump on him, or easier access to the pyramid. Let's see what they're up to."

Edgar's face betrayed no enthusiasm for the idea. "You first."

The warriors climbed the steps to the playing field and advanced to the pyramid. When they were out of sight, Rick dashed out of his hiding place and ran up the right side of the steps so that the viewing stands blocked their view of him. Edgar followed, but stayed at the base of the steps.

The warriors went to the end of the field and manhandled the deposed chief up to the base of the pyramid steps in front of the ash-filled firepit. They forced him to his knees and the new chief stood before him. He smacked the deposed chief across the face with the skull staff, opening a gash along his cheek. Then he ripped the jaguar neckpiece from him. With great ceremony, he bent it into a ball and threw it in the firepit. It hit the ash and sent up a cloud of black dust.

The new chief pronounced a few vindictive-sounding sentences. Then he traded his skull staff for a spear from one of the warriors. With a single thrust, he drove it into the prisoner's chest. The victim screamed and grabbed the spear's shaft. The chief jammed it in deeper, until it exited through the man's back. When the chief released the spear, the prisoner fell dead.

The chief barked an order to the two warriors carrying the stone posts. They came forward and climbed the pyramid steps to the top, followed by two others. Then they began to raise and drop the posts against the top step until it crumbled into pieces. When it had shattered, they moved down and went to work on the next step.

The other two warriors gathered the broken pieces and started wedging them into the opening at the pyramid summit. It looked like not only were these people done making offerings to the vampire, they were done even letting him leave the pyramid.

Someone could still get to the top of the pyramid if they wanted to, but this new chief was doing something symbolic. The execution of the chief would cement his leadership role. The crushing of the jaguar neckpiece and the destruction of the sacrificial steps said more than that. The man was repudiating the worship of Itztli, the sacrifice of their women, the veneration of this dead city and the undead within it.

"Why couldn't you have stepped up before Rose was kidnapped?" Rick said to himself.

He hurried down the steps to where Edgar waited hidden in the shadows of the playing field.

"The chief is dead," Rick said. "Long live the chief."

"Bloody unstable form of government these chaps have."

"And they're breaking up the stairs leading to the summit. We're not getting in that way. We need to stick with our original plan."

"The crawling through a jaguar tunnel plan? Just peachy."

The two of them descended into the ruins and skirted the edge of the playing field until they came back to where they'd hidden in the collapsed building. Rick spotted the opening in the pyramid and led Edgar to it.

Rick took the silver finger guards from his pocket and put them on. The fit was poor, but considering what he had to work with, the best he could expect. Each piece extended to or past his second knuckle, which immobilized his fingers and meant he wouldn't be grasping anything with his left hand. That was probably all the better if his left hand was going to be an anti-vampire weapon.

"Okay," Rick said. "In we go."

"What if a jaguar decides to follow us in?"

"It's daylight. They're only out at night."

"What if those warriors we just left on the field decide to poke about looking for us? They'll see our footprints leading to this hole. They'll either follow us in or seal it closed and then we'll be in there with the vampire forever."

"I'm getting my wife out of that pyramid."

"As well you should. How about I stand guard out here? That will keep inquisitive wildlife away. If any warriors come by, I'll shout you a warning down the passage, then lead them off in another direction. We're both saved instead of both being trapped."

While Rick was certain Edgar's plan was born out of complete cowardice, it might just provide the extra level of safety they'd need. With Rose's life in the balance, he'd exploit every chance to turn this longshot bet into a sure thing.

"Okay," Rick said. "You stand guard here. Sing out if anyone shows up."

"Jolly good." Edgar reached in his pocket and pulled out a handkerchief wrapped around something. He unfolded it to reveal three silver tips. "Take these. The vampire is in there. You'll need them more than I will."

Rick was touched. He might have to re-evaluate Edgar's character after all.

"Even better," Edgar said. "Give me your extra silver as well. Might as well concentrate the power in one place."

"Good idea." Rick took out his three silver tips and gave them to Edgar.

Edgar wrapped both sets in his handkerchief. He flattened out the lump, slid it into his pocket, and then took it back out. "There, not too bulky. He'll feel the power, but be quite flummoxed over where you're hiding it."

"Thanks." Rick took the handkerchief and put it in his own pocket. "See you in a few minutes."

"I'll be here."

Rick stuck his head into the tunnel. There was only darkness ahead. He wished he still had one of the flashlights. He got a good whiff of the air. It stank of jaguar urine. Rose had damn well better appreciate this.

He squeezed into the tunnel. If he angled his body, he could crawl forward with his shoulders scraping the upper right and lower left corners. Sub-optimal to say the least. But it beat climbing the pyramid and knocking on the door at the top.

He sighed and moved forward away from the light.

***

Edgar watched until the darkness swallowed the soles of Rick's shoes.

"What a twit," he said to himself.

There was no way in hell he was going to stand outside this pyramid waiting to be killed by a wild animal, a warrior, or both. He needed to be out of this godforsaken country immediately and there was an airplane on the river ready to make that happen.

He pulled a folded handkerchief from his pocket. Opening it revealed his and Rick's consecrated silver tips. Edgar had hit him with an old grifting trick and switched out the handkerchief full of silver for one filled with stones. Rick returning alive, especially with his wife, meant more people who might come back to this city before he did and take any treasure here for themselves.

He laughed and dropped the silver pieces and the handkerchief on the ground.

Silver was chump change. He patted his pockets. Still full. In the melee at the end of the battle reenactment, he'd stripped an unconscious warrior of his gold gauntlets and necklaces. He wouldn't return to England a rich man, but he'd have a good start. Combined with inheriting his father's house, he could avoid stooping to have a paying job for several years. When he ran low, he'd come back here and make another withdrawal from the Bank of Tezpaluca.

Then Edgar turned and ran. He made his way through the ruins until he could get a good look at the playing field again. Busy warriors crushed steps under the chief's supervision, making this the perfect time for a clean getaway.

He ran for the main road and the path back through the jungle. If he hurried, he'd make it to the plane by midday, and he could be back in Cuba for dinner.

CHAPTER THIRTY-TWO

The passage into the pyramid was damn tight.

As Rick crawled forward in total darkness, he wondered why this shaft was here. It wasn't designed for people to use, and while it seemed Itztli had recruited the jaguars to use it for home delivery services, the builders certainly hadn't been planning for telepathic vampires to be entombed here. His best guess was that it was for ventilation, with the pyramid acting like a giant chimney to the structure at its peak.

Rick wasn't prone to being claustrophobic, but this little journey was threatening to make him a convert. The bottom of the shaft felt slimy, and he was glad he couldn't see what he was resting his hands in. His cock-eyed, arm-first crawl through the passage reinforced how tight the space was with every bump and scrape against the stone walls. The humid air stank of all scents jaguar, especially a musky grade of ammonia that made the air miserable to breathe. The icing on the claustrophobia cake was thinking that tens of thousands of pounds of rock sat overhead, ready and waiting to collapse and crush him.

The further forward he moved, the more worried he became. He thought he should have seen some of the light-at-the-end-of-the-tunnel people always spoke about. Since he hadn't, that might mean that the room he'd exit into wasn't lit. That was a reasonable possibility since vampires only worked at night, so they could probably see in the dark far better than humans. If that was true, he'd be at a distinct disadvantage trying to find Rose and get her out of here.

The other, and worse reason he didn't see any light would be that the tunnel made a sharp curve, one that the flexible spine of a big cat could navigate, but the rigid spine of a person could not. That would force him to back out of the tunnel, and he wasn't even sure he could do that.

Time seemed to slow to quarter speed, measured only by the scrape of his skin against the shaft walls. Simultaneously, he knew that every moment of delay was a moment something awful could happen to Rose. This combination only made him even more anxious. His heart was pounding so hard he thought he could hear it echo in the shaft.

Then he made a discovery so dire he hadn't considered it possible. His hands touched a wall at the end of the shaft.

Sweat dripped down his face. He probed the edges with his fingertips and found nothing but the right-angles where stone met stone. The shaft had been dark because it was a dead end. On the other side of this block, his wife was captive to a vampire, and he couldn't do anything about it.

He pushed back his emotional reaction and tried to think this revelation through. A dead end made no sense. The builders wouldn't build one, plus he'd seen the jaguars enter with food and come out without any. Since there wasn't a pile of peccaries here, they had to have been delivered to the pyramid's interior.

So, this couldn't be a wall. It had to be a door.

But how to open it?

He'd felt no latches, no grips to pull it open, not that a cat was going to turn a knob to open a door anyway. Now that he thought of it, how would a cat open a door?

House cats he'd seen at home were pretty adept at pushing doors open with their foreheads.

He was willing to try anything before quitting and backing out. He crawled forward until the top of his head rested against the end of the shaft. He doubted he had the physical strength of a jaguar, but he'd give it all he had. He braced his hands and feet against the sides of the shaft, took a deep breath of the rank, thick air, and pushed.

The muscles in his neck bulged. His spine compressed under the strain. The rough surface of the stone ground into his scalp.

And the block didn't move.

He stopped and exhaled hard.

"If a damn cat can do this, so can I."

Rick took several deep breaths, and tried again. As he grunted against the rock, he imagined his blood vessels straining to the bursting point.

Then the rock moved. It slid forward a few inches, and then sideways all by itself. Light flooded the shaft. It wasn't overly bright, but given how long he'd been in total darkness, it momentarily blinded Rick. His eyes adapted.

He reached forward, grabbed the edges of this new opening, and pulled himself out of the shaft. He arrived in a shadowy corridor. A look at the stone he'd moved revealed that once pushed out, it slid down an angled slope from its own weight to clear the shaft. There was a lever at the bottom of the slope. Perhaps the weight of the jaguar in retreat moved that lever to close the stone door again.

Rick stood and shook off the muscle cramps the tiny shaft had induced. He gave the four finger gauntlets on his left hand a check. Then he took off his belt and wedged it into the track for the stone door. No point risking this thing shutting on him before he and Rose were out of here.

Then with his back against one wall, he made his way to the lighted end of the corridor. The passage opened to a huge room. He gave the place a once-over from the shadows.

This had to be the pyramid's center. The circular room was about thirty feet across. A ring of nooks filled the wall below a shelf filled with golden treasures. Some kind of stone altar stood in the center and above it glowed an egg-shaped crystal that seemed to light the room, though there were lamps burning in the walls as well. But the most important feature in the room took all his attention.

Rose sat on the floor directly across from him, shackled to an eyelet with a heavy chain.

Rick's heart soared. Rose was alive, just as he'd hoped. No, just as he'd *known* since the moment she'd disappeared into the pyramid. As sure as he'd been that she was here, he was just as sure that now he'd get her out. There was the little problem of the chain that shackled her to the floor, but if the chain went on, the chain could come off. That was just a minor detail he'd solve in a minute.

He pulled the packet of silver tips that Edgar had given him from his pocket and unfolded the handkerchief.

Inside were several stones.

"That rat," Rick whispered. Edgar had lied and set him up to feel a lot more protected going into the vampire's den than he really was. Any illusions about that little liar still guarding the shaft's exit were dispelled. But Rick would have to worry about that later. Right now, he had to get Rose.

He still had the finger gauntlets. He checked that they were as tight as possible over the fingers of his left hand. He offered up a prayer that this would be enough silver to keep a vampire at bay.

He gave the room another inspection. Itztli wasn't there. Probably tending to whatever vampire business vampires tended to inside Aztec pyramids. Rick didn't care what it was as long as it took long enough for him to get Rose out of bondage and far away.

Rick stepped into the light of the corridor threshold. Rose was staring at one of the walls, as if studying the inscriptions under the openings.

Leave it to Rose to be kidnapped by a vampire and still be fascinated by some nuggets of history, he thought.

He decided an understated, Hollywood-cool, Errol Flynn kind of entrance would be in order here. He leaned against one side of the threshold, grinned, and gave Rose a casual wave with one hand.

That caught her attention. Her face lit up with surprise. Then her eyes narrowed. She bit her lower lip.

Rick rushed out into the room. He was about to call out to her when he heard the rustling of cloth above him. He whirled around with the altar just to his back.

Itztli plummeted down from the stairway over that side of the room. His cape flapped behind him like the plumage of a great bird of prey. The impact of that kind of drop would have shattered a man's legs. But Itztli landed hard on his heels with only the barest flex of his knees. His cape dropped behind him like a theatre curtain and the lower two tips came forward to wrap inside his calves.

With his hood swept back, Rick got his first close view of the creature that had taken his wife, and every feature sent chill bumps up his arms. Pale skin, pointed features, and worst of all, rows of sharp teeth and a pair of outsized fangs.

"What a surprise," Itztli said. "My dinner is delivered."

CHAPTER THIRTY-THREE

Rose fumed at how much worse her situation had just become. She had almost worked the eyelet of her shackles out of the floor. Rick's welcome but early arrival came before she was able to run. And with Itztli now blocking his escape, Rick wasn't either.

Rick rolled over the altar and landed on his feet at Rose's side.

"Maybe you could tell me there's a vampire over my head?" he said.

"I did. I gave you the look."

"That was your 'I'm glad to see you' look."

"It was not. And after this fiasco you'll be lucky to ever see *that* look again."

Itztli stepped up to the other side of the altar and sprouted a malevolent grin, which his teeth made even more ghoulish.

"Don't tell me you think you came to her rescue?" Itztli said.

Rose guessed Rick could hear Itztli's telepathy as well as she did.

"That's exactly the plan," Rick said. "Now you went and spoiled the surprise."

Itztli ran a bony finger around the edge of the altar. "Here's what's going to happen instead. I'm going to break your arms and legs. One at a time. Slowly. Then I'm going to lay you out here on my dinner table and slowly drain you of every drop of blood, savoring it to the last. What's left will be food for the jaguars."

"Here's a counter-offer," Rick said. "We all walk up to the top of the pyramid, you let us go, and I don't kill you."

Rose had no idea how Rick thought he'd pull that off. She hoped this wasn't one of the times he was bluffing, because she knew Itztli was not.

"You cannot kill one who is immortal, and I will never release the future mother of my son."

Rick spun around with a panicked look on his face. "Rose, did he—"

"No!" Rose directed the next sentence to Itztli. "And he never will."

"She's already married," Rick said to Itztli. "And she takes the vows seriously. So, she's not available for spawning demons."

With only the barest flex of his knees, Itztli leapt up onto the altar. Rick took one shocked step backward.

"Consent is not required. I was going to wait, but now I have a new plan. Once your broken body is on the table here, I'll let you watch the first time I take her. It's going to be painful for her, but she'll get used to it."

Anger flared in Rick's eyes. He brought his left hand back and Rose noticed that his fingers all hosted a shiny metal covering. Her heart leapt as she realized her husband had come armed with silver. Leave it to Rick to stack the odds in his favor.

Rick sprinted for the altar, and with a broad swipe, slashed Itztli's leg. Four parallel wounds gaped open in Itztli's calf. The vampire screamed and dropped to one knee.

Rose wondered how long it had been since Itztli had felt real pain. She was glad Rick had been the one to deliver it.

Rick reared back for a second attack. But Itztli wasn't waiting for that to happen. One hand shot out and he grabbed Rick by the throat. Rick choked as the vampire lifted him off the floor. Then Itztli tossed him up over the altar and against the far wall. Rick hit with a thud that made Rose wince, and then he slid down to the floor.

Itztli hopped off the altar and faced Rick. The wounds on the vampire's leg were already healing. The silver claws could at best just buy them time. With Itztli looking in the other direction, she began to kick at the eyelet with both feet, praying she'd free herself before Itztli finished off her husband.

Rick stood, the look on his face much more wary as Itztli approached.

"You had no idea how powerful Tezcatlipoca had made his followers, did you?" Itztli said. "And how stupid and futile it would be to enter my pyramid?"

"This pyramid is about to become a tomb," Rick said.

"Yes," Itztli said. "But it will be *your* tomb."

Itztli rushed at Rick, hands aiming for his throat again. At the last second, Rick ducked. Itztli's hands hit the wall hard enough to crunch stone. Rick drove his clawed fingers up and into the vampire's chest. Itztli shrieked and recoiled. Rick dug in harder.

Itztli growled in response. Fury blazed in his eyes. He reached down and pulled Rick's hand from his chest like he was pulling out a splinter. He dragged Rick backward. As he did, he spun him around by his wrist, lifted him up, and brought him crashing down on the altar back first like a flipped pancake. Rick hit with a thud and a crunch that sounded like bones.

Rose winced at her husband's pain. She kicked harder at the eyelet.

"You can't win," Itztli said. "The power of Tezcatlipoca has made me immortal. The Spanish Empire couldn't kill me. You certainly can't. Now lie still."

Itztli released Rick's wrist, raised a fist, and brought it down on Rick's leg. This time the crack of bone was loud and clear. Rick wailed.

Itztli put his face inches from Rick's. "That's one down and three to go."

Rick cocked his left hand, stuck his fingers straight out, and then rammed them claws-first straight into the vampire's mouth. The creature's teeth raked bloody slashes across Rick's hand but he kept pushing.

Itztli's eyes went wide. He gagged and stepped back, clawing at his mouth.

Rose finally kicked the eyelet free. A chunk of stone still encased the shaft, but she was free. She smiled and stood. It was time to make exterminating this vermin a team effort.

She grabbed her shackle and spun the heavy eyelet at the end around over her head like a cowboy with a lasso. Rose aimed at the Mooncatcher. When it shattered, the curtain would come down on Itztli's show. Alive and powerless was as good as dead as far as she was concerned.

She released the chain and the eyelet at the end arced through the air. It struck the Mooncatcher and the crystal shattered. White light flashed so brightly that the room was lit to every corner. Shards rained down like a hailstorm of frosted glass. She covered her face.

When the cascade stopped, Rose lowered her hands, expecting the remaining oil lamp lights to reveal a prone and weakened Itztli on the floor.

The vampire still stood. He shook to shed the crystal shards from his head and shoulders. He hacked and pulled three bloody claws from his mouth with his fingers. He dropped them by the altar. He hacked again, and then spit the fourth claw out at Rose. It landed by her feet.

"Is the word immortal unclear to you two?" He laughed. "Did you think the Mooncatcher was some source of power? Humans are so stupid."

He grabbed the eyelet end of the chain and cracked it like a whip. The end with her shackle jerked up high and hard. It swept her off her feet and she landed flat on her back. Itztli wrapped the end of the chain around his wrist.

"Killing your husband will now take longer than I'd planned," he said. "And I'm going to enjoy every minute of it."

CHAPTER THIRTY-FOUR

"That there's a work of art," Humphrey said to himself. "Just need to tighten up these wires."

He stood beside the open cowling of the left side Liberty engine. He'd found the burned-up ignition wire. Well, he'd found *a* burned-up ignition wire. Was that the only problem this under-maintained aircraft had? He doubted it. But he hoped it was the only one that was keeping the plane grounded. Carlos would have to take care of the rest of the deferred maintenance when this crate got back to Cuba.

And there'd be more problems than just the mechanical. Down below him, the damn termite fish were going at the hull like hogs at a slop trough. There were almost as many now as there had been when he hosted the First Annual Mexican Fish Fry a few hours ago. A second round of that was out of the question, so Rick and Rose needed to get back here before the hull became a river water strainer.

"I say there! Start that aeroplane!"

The panicked cry with a British accent came from the riverbank. A portly, disheveled stranger in khaki clothing stood there waving both arms. Humphrey hadn't expected to see anyone other than Rick and the others on the riverbank, and he certainly didn't expect to see someone from England.

"That boy is on the wrong side of the world," Humphrey said.

The man glanced up and down the riverbank until he spotted the Aeromarine's raft. He dragged it into the water and began a wild, splashing paddle to the plane that produced more foam than forward motion.

"Start the bloody engines!" the man shouted between strokes. "They're coming!"

Since he'd ended his Air Corps service, Humphrey had acquired an aversion to following orders, especially from strangers.

"Who the hell are you?"

The raft came close enough that the man didn't have to shout. "Edgar Dartmouth. I'm here doing research with my father. We were working with your friends, Rick and Rose."

At the sound of those names, Humphrey's curiosity, as well as his suspicions peaked. "Where are they?"

Edgar bumped the nose of the raft against the airplane's hull. The termite fish at that spot scattered. "I'm afraid they're dead. All perished, save myself."

The news hit Humphrey like a gut punch. "All of them?"

"Even my father. The villagers rounded us all up. They sacrificed the others at a pyramid in the jungle. I managed an escape but there's a group of warriors right behind me."

The Lost City found. Native warriors in the jungle. Everyone who flew in with him dead. The stranger just dumped more information than Humphrey could sort through in an instant.

The man climbed out of the raft and it began to drift away. Humphrey grabbed the rope at the bow and lashed it to the hull. The termite fish had already returned to that spot and were hard at work again.

"How do you know they're dead if you escaped?" he said.

"I saw it all happen. Not a pretty sight, I assure you. I was quite lucky to get away with my life."

Having lived his life on the ragged edge of honesty meant Humphrey had become expert on sensing when someone else was doing the same. Edgar here was too flippant about the details. In the war, Humphrey had met dozens of people who'd narrowly dodged death. They were more likely to tell you about it in detail than to gloss over it like Edgar was doing.

He gave Edgar a closer inspection. No cuts or scrapes. No bruises. Nothing said he'd fought his way out against a band of savages. His pockets bulged with odd shapes, all sharp edges, and the weight was enough to make his pants sag hard against his belt. Even the most backward native would empty the pockets of their foreign prisoners, even if only out of curiosity. The man looked more like a thief than a victim right now.

"Y'all found the City of Gold?"

"What? Don't be silly. There's nothing here but jungle and natives with poisoned arrows. And we'll be catching some if we don't push on out of here now."

Humphrey cocked an ear to the jungle. He heard nothing but insects. One Englishman bashing through the jungle wouldn't leave local expert warriors so far behind.

"There's nothing there? You just said you were at a pyramid."

"Yes, more like a pile of abandoned rocks, I suppose. I'm not an archaeologist and I was too scared to pay attention to anything but the damn broadswords at my throat."

Humphrey was pretty sure an undiscovered tribe in the Mexican jungle wouldn't be smelting themselves broadswords. This boy's story was starting to stink six ways from Sunday.

"How did you know I was here with the plane?"

"Rick told me. The last thing he said to me was 'Edgar, the plane is on the river. Get to it and make sure Humphrey saves himself and tells our children what happened out here.'"

The Sinclair were many things, but the one thing they definitely weren't were parents. Humphrey grabbed Edgar, dragged him into the cabin and threw him down into a chair.

"Now, boy, why don't you tell me what the hell is really going on here."

"You're right. There's gold." Edgar reached into a pocket and pulled out what looked like a gold wristlet. "And silver. Lots of it there, and I'm loaded up with it now. A fortune to split between us, fifty-fifty. Plus, you can keep this plane. But first things first, we need to get the hell out of here."

Humphrey spit on the deck. "I ain't going nowhere without Rick and Rose."

Edgar leapt from the chair with remarkable speed. He caught Humphrey off guard, drove a shoulder into his chest, and slammed him against the cabin wall. Then he stepped back and sent a right cross against Humphrey's chin.

Humphrey's head whipped around and smacked into the cabin wall. Everything flashed to white and his head seemed to spin like a top. He slumped down to the deck and passed out.

CHAPTER THIRTY-FIVE

Rose had been in some tough scrapes with Rick before, but this looked like the one they couldn't escape. Itztli held the chain attached to her ankle and Rick was incapacitated on the altar. The wounds on Itztli's leg were completely healed. There was no way she and Rick were going to get out of this pyramid alive now.

At least not without help.

She thought that maybe there *was* some help, help that Itztli himself had revealed to her.

The glyph in the altar top was that of Itztli, the same one she'd seen all over the city and pyramid. But it did not match the one on the empty tomb where Itztli belonged. That glyph was under the opening of a hibernating vampire just to her right. Itztli inferred that he couldn't trust all the royal members in the walls. That would make sense if he wasn't Itztli at all, and the vampire in that niche with the Itztli glyph was.

She guessed that vampire would like a little revenge on the one who usurped his name and his throne. All she had to do was wake him up.

She had a terrible idea of how to do that.

As Itztli dropped her chain and staggered over to resume Rick's torture on the altar, Rose grabbed the finger claw the vampire had spit at her feet. She slashed the palm of her left hand. The crude blade made a ragged cut. Sharp, immediate pain radiated up to her elbow.

Bright red blood ran from the wound. She dashed over to the vampire over the Itztli hieroglyph. The chain of her shackles rattled against the stone floor behind her.

The noise garnered Itztli's attention. "What are you doing?"

She reached the opening and stuck her bleeding hand inside. The recess smelled of decay and must with a repulsive overlay of death. She clamped her palm across the vampire's lips. The creature's skin felt like dried papier mâché over bone.

Itztli realized what she was doing. "No! Stop!"

As her blood touched the vampire's lips, she felt them swell and warm. They pursed and sucked blood from her palm, faster than it was bleeding. It was as if a vacuum had been turned on inside her veins. The vampire's withered hand whipped up and pressed hers hard against his face. Color returned to the creature's skin. Warmth radiated from the body and out the opening.

Itztli ran to Rose. He grabbed her around the waist, pulled her free of the other vampire's grip and tossed her across the room.

He was too late. The new vampire shot one arm out, struck Itztli in the back, and sent him reeling. Then the creature pulled himself from the crypt and onto his feet. This new vampire stood a half-foot taller that Itztli, and renewed by Rose's blood, looked much more robust. He only wore a loincloth, but around his neck hung a copy of the same neckpiece the village chief had worn. He looked down at Itztli with unbridled anger.

"Ahuatzi, you traitorous snake," the true Itztli said. "How dare you take my name and pretend to rule with Tezcatlipoca's favor."

Rose could hear the vampire clearly in her head. He wasn't speaking to her but he sounded so mad that she guessed this was the equivalent of telepathic shouting.

Ahuatzi cowered. "I was about to wake you with this human's blood."

"Liar. As you have always been a liar. We immortals may be physically dormant in these walls but we are mentally awake. All you have done I have heard, and every century you have kept me sleeping I have endured."

Ahuatzi dropped the meek persona and squared his shoulders. "And it's where you should be. Tezcatlipoca made a mistake making you the leader. Your weakness brought the Spanish and their sorcerer priests to our city streets, and it allowed them to seal us in this prison. You don't deserve to rule."

"And traitors don't deserve to live."

The risen Itztli charged Ahuatzi. They crashed into the wall so hard that stone crushed into dust behind them. Then they began fighting. The vampires' speed and power made the event almost a blur as the two careened back and forth across the room.

Rose went to Rick and helped him sit up. "Can you walk?"

"With your help, I can do anything."

Rose assisted him off the altar. She coiled her chain and slung it across one shoulder. Rick draped his arm across her other and tried not to put any weight on his broken leg. She half-dragged him in the direction of the corridor.

The two vampires wrestled back and forth. As Rose hobbled across the room, the two came barreling in her direction. Rick saw them as well. They dodged left and the vampires brushed by them.

They entered the corridor, which was almost all shadow now that Rose had smashed the Mooncatcher. Rick looked back at the gold treasures along the wall.

"Don't even think about it," Rose said.

"Rosie, just one of those plates are worth a fortune."

"And none are worth our lives. So how was it you got in here, anyway?"

"Some kind of ventilation shaft. Up here on the left."

Indeed, a few yards up a tight, rectangular hole gaped in the wall. Rose eased Rick down beside it. From the room behind them came the roar of a furious vampire. Rose wondered which one was getting the worst of it. No matter who won, the two of them would be losers if they were still here at the end of the fight.

"You go first," Rose said.

"No, it had better be you. I'll need your help getting out on the other side."

Rose stuck her head inside and got a whiff of the stink. "This smells like a litter box."

"Wait until you feel how slimy it is, then you'll really love it."

In the big room, one vampire screamed at a pitch that meant some serious damage had been done. Rose wondered if being immortal was worse in a fight like that, where one could endure a cycle of being wounded and healing for all eternity.

"Hurry," Rick said. "If one of them goes down, the victor will be after us in a second."

Rose climbed into the shaft. A bit of light at the far end promised that indeed they could escape. Rick had been right. The floor of the shaft felt awfully slimy. She wished she had a clothespin to clamp shut her nose. With as little breathing and as rapid a crawl as possible, she headed down the shaft, dragging the chain with her. Her shoulders scraped the walls and she wondered how her larger husband had made it through the first time.

She heard Rick moan. Unable to look over her shoulder, she looked back between her legs. All she saw was darkness.

"Are you okay?" she said.

"I'll make it. Keep moving."

Rose scrambled down the shaft and finally reached blessed daylight and fresh air at the end. She crawled out and ended up doing a cockeyed somersault on exit with her chain following behind. She jumped back up, wiped her hands clean against her pants and went back to the shaft. She pulled the rest of her chain out of the pyramid. Looking in, she saw that Rick was just out of reach.

"Hurry," she said.

"You're going to have to help me," Rick said.

He crawled forward until Rose could grab his hands.

"Pull, like you're uncorking a bottle of wine," Rick said. "A fine wine, by the way."

"This one might have aged past its prime. We'll see."

Rose braced her feet against the wall and pulled. Rick's head emerged into the daylight with him lying on his back. When he was out to his waist, she went back to the opening and eased his body out and onto the ground. He stifled a scream of pain, then exhaled and sat up.

A handkerchief and several of the silver tips from the encircling ring caught her eye by the pyramid wall. She picked one up. "How did this get here?"

"The rat Edgar." Rick searched around and picked up several more tips. "He gave me the old switcharoo and instead of sending me in with a vampire repellent, let me go in there defenseless. He was also supposed to be waiting here for us to return. I'll bet he's headed for the plane, and no good will come of that."

"We'd better hurry, then."

"First, let's make this pyramid the sealed tomb it's supposed to be. We'll block this shaft so jaguars can't get in."

"The vampires still won't die," Rose said, "but at least they'll all go dormant without the peccary blood offerings. But first things first, let's splint your leg for the trip out of here."

Rose found two mostly straight sticks and Rick shredded his shirt. They bound up his leg and gave Rick some immediate relief from the worst of the pain. Then Rose collected broken blocks from the collapsed building and brought them to Rick, who worked them into a tight block in the ventilation shaft. He wedged the silver tips into positions between the rocks.

"If one of the vampires climbs up the shaft to clear it out," Rick said, "these ought to work like land mines."

"And jaguars won't be able to paw those rocks out," Rose said, "no matter what Itztli or Ahuatzi tell them to do."

"And they won't be back for hours. I watched direct sunlight bake one like a potato, so I bet they cat nap all day until nightfall."

"But some other girl will still be the next victim. The villagers will still be making offerings to whichever vampire survives."

"Not from what we saw at the pyramid steps," Rick said. "The tribe is under new management again, and this chief seems to have had enough of vampire worship. The villagers blocked the entrance at the top so no vampires get out."

"You said *we saw*. What happened to the professor?"

"He didn't make it," Rick said. "I wish it had been Edgar instead. Here's hoping the villagers caught Edgar."

"If they haven't," Rose said, "I hope he can't find his way back to the plane."

"More important," Rick said, "I hope *we* can."

***

In the bowels of the pyramid, Ahuatzi lay battered and broken on the floor beside the altar. The fresh infusion of the woman's blood had made Itztli physically more powerful than peccary blood could have ever made Ahuatzi. Itztli's long-simmering fury over his usurpation had fueled a relentless assault. Now Ahuatzi lay in a pool of blood. His crushed ribcage had punctured many organs. His dislocated jaw hung at a painful, awful angle. He'd shattered a wrist ramming his fist into Itztli's skull. Eventually, all the injuries would heal, but it would take a lot of time and a lot of peccary blood.

Ahuatzi turned his head to see his rival. His only consolation was that Itztli hadn't finished the fight unscathed. A hodgepodge of scrapes and bruises painted the ruler's body. He limped heavily, favoring a bloody left foot. A swath of his scalp hung over one ear, exposing white bone. Itztli leaned against the wall by his crypt, panting. The fight had been a draw.

"In any century," Ahuatzi said, "you are no match for me. All that held me back before was that the others were too cowardly to stand behind me."

"It was that the others could not stomach standing *beside* a coward, a man who could only steal the throne he could not earn."

Ahuatzi pushed his jaw back into place and managed a triumphant look. "We will heal, but I will heal faster. Jaguars respond to my commands and will bring me blood, guard me while my bones knit and my flesh mends. You will watch me grow stronger while you grow weaker. Soon I will rise and stuff you back into your hole in the wall. My only regret is there isn't a way to kill you instead."

Itztli smiled. Blood stained his teeth. "You may pretend to be me, but you do not know my secrets."

Itztli turned around and slipped his hands into recesses in the stone that contained his hieroglyph. He pulled it out and it was only an inch or so thick. He turned about and revealed its reverse to Ahuatzi. Four silver spikes protruded from the stone.

Ahuatzi's heart skipped a beat. One of the few fatal injuries for a vampire was too many simultaneous, silver impalings. Four spikes driven into the wrong location, and his life was over.

"Remember all my rivals who disappeared over the years?" Itztli said. "I crushed their heads with this. Their blood still stains the blades. Now your blood will mingle with theirs."

Ahuatzi cursed. All these centuries, the weapon had been hidden. If only he had known, he could have finished the slumbering Itztli long ago. Instead, he was going to be its victim.

Ahuatzi tried to move, tried to just raise an arm in his own defense. His broken body refused to respond.

Itztli staggered over and stopped at Ahuatzi's side. He raised the block over Ahuatzi's head. The tip of one blade hung a few inches over Ahuatzi's right eye.

His centuries of struggle and solitude had been wasted, his dream of ruling a resurgent Tezcatlipoca destroyed. He had no escape, but he could deal an enemy one final blow.

He closed his eyes and sent out a final command to a jaguar minion.

Kill the two who escaped the pyramid.

And then Ahuatzi thought no more.

CHAPTER THIRTY-SIX

Rick directed Rose through the ruins to where the old Aztec road led into the city.

"The fastest and surest way to the river is this trail," Rick said, "and it bypasses the village."

"I'm carrying fifty pounds of chains and you're walking as well as a drunken sailor," Rose said. "I'm not sure we have another choice."

"And we already know where the giant spiders are, so we can apply guanabana before we get there. The old road is the way to go."

"And if the warriors hunting us think the same thing?"

"Let's hope they don't," Rick said.

The trip down the trail was much slower going than Rose had hoped. They did manage to dab on some guanabana and circle the worst of the spider traps. On the other side, the Spanish armor they'd discovered earlier still sat under the tree where they'd left it.

Rick gave it a longing look. "Rosie?"

"Oh no. Don't you even consider trying to take that home."

"We already left all that gold behind in the pyramid."

"No," Rose said. "We'll be lucky to get out of here alive as it is."

"But we're going home empty-handed. That silver armor would turn a nice profit."

"We can't carry all that."

"I'll wear it."

Rose shook her head. "I can barely support you now."

"Okay, then a helmet. I'll wear that. You don't want to go home with no proof any of this happened. And that professor at the college would pay big bucks for it, I'm sure."

Rose considered the idea. "Fine, the helmet. But don't complain about how heavy it is later."

"As long as you don't complain when the proceeds from it pay off our debt and put a new roof on the shop."

Rick balanced on one leg as Rose retrieved a helmet. Rick donned it. It was a bit small and kind of sat on his head like a beanie.

"You look ridiculous," she said.

"If by ridiculous you mean wealthy, then you're dead right. Let's go home."

An hour later, Rick and Rose entered a part of the old road that ran through a virtual tunnel of trees. About ten feet up, branches stretched out from both sides to block the unrelenting tropical sun. The jungle off to each side was also all darkness and shadow. Rose didn't like the look of it at all.

"This is the kind of place the Grimm Brothers set their fairy tales," Rose said as she helped Rick limp down the overgrown pavers.

"Fantastic!" Rick said. "I could snack on a gingerbread house about now."

"I'm serious. We've seen plenty of dangerous animals, not to mention the tribal hunters. Any of them could be lying in ambush and we're defenseless."

"We're the least of the tribe's worries right now. The jaguars only hunt at night. We left the spiders way behind us. From here on out it's smooth sailing, Rosie."

"But if anyone, or anything is after us, they'll assume we'll take this trail."

"This is the shortest route to the flying boat," Rick said. "And I'm not up for anything but the shortest route at this point. We'll be at the riverbank in no time."

Rose shook her head. "You have a knack for optimism that is both unbridled and unsupported."

"And unassailable. When have I ever steered you wrong?"

"As soon as I'm not using one hand to keep you from falling down and the other to hold this damn chain, I'll make you a list."

Off to the left, leaves rustled.

"Did you hear that?" Rose said.

"I'm still too distraught over your lack of faith in me to hear anything."

Leaves rustled again. Rose paused walking. Rick lurched to a stop beside her.

"You had to have heard that," she said.

"Afraid I did." Rick eased out of the grip Rose had around his waist and leaned against a tree trunk.

More leaf litter stirred to the left, closer, and louder this time. Rose's pulse quickened.

Then a peccary burst out of the jungle and onto the trail. It executed a comical skid across the pavers until its claws caught in a clump of moss. It quickly righted itself and disappeared into the jungle on the other side.

"See," Rick said, "nothing to worry about."

Rose wasn't mollified. The peccary had to be running from something.

From the darkness under low hanging leaves on the left, a pair of yellow eyes opened.

Before Rose could respond, a jaguar leapt out of the shadows, aimed straight at the two of them.

Rick pushed Rose to the left and then dropped down to the right. The jaguar sailed between them. The weight of the chain in her hands made Rose topple to the ground. She hit the pavers hard enough to make her teeth rattle. Rick teetered on his one good leg and then he went down as well. The conquistador helmet fell off his head and hit the stones with a clang.

The jaguar skidded to a stop and spat out a frustrated growl. It spun around and crouched. Its eyes whipped back and forth between Rick and Rose. Maybe it sensed the male of the duo was a greater threat. Maybe it thought the injured human the easier target. For whatever reason, it locked its eyes on Rick and pounced.

Rick grabbed the helmet by the crest with both hands. He got it in front of his chest, open end up, just as the jaguar landed. Its forepaws straddled Rick's shoulders, its hind paws his ankles. It snarled and spittle splattered Rick's cheeks. Rick locked his elbows. The helmet held the jaguar at bay, but just inches from Rick's face.

Rose went to her knees. The side of her body ached where she'd hit the pavers. She stood and caught the jaguar's attention. It hissed in her direction and then snapped at Rick again. Her husband's trembling arms threatened to buckle.

She spied the chain that lay at her feet. She could hit the cat with it, but she wouldn't kill it. Then it would kill her, and then kill Rick before he could limp away on his splinted leg. She just didn't have the strength to take on the big cat.

But she knew what did. Rick had told her the jaguar's greatest weakness.

She scanned the trees for the optimal branch. Once she saw it, she jumped to her feet with the chain coiled in her hand. With all her strength, she reared back, aimed, and sent the chain soaring through the air. The chain passed over the branch and uncoiled on the other side with the eyelet dangling eight feet off the ground.

Rose ran for that end. The eyelet, her only hope to save her husband, swayed like a clock's pendulum, marking the seconds left in Rick's life. As she closed on it, the eyelet seemed impossibly out of reach, her arms too short to grab it, the leg iron too heavy to jump for it. She gritted her teeth and leapt.

Her fingers grazed the eyelet. She grabbed both strands of chain with both hands, tucked up her legs, and let gravity and her body weight do the work.

The branch sagged, and then snapped. Rose landed on her butt. Falling chain snaked into a sloppy coil atop her waist.

The fallen branch revealed a patch of blue sky. A shaft of sunlight hit Rick and the jaguar like a spotlight.

The jaguar howled in pain. Smoke rose from its fur. It stood full up on all fours. The stench of cooked, rotten meat filled the air.

Rick acted fast. With the helmet free, he spun it around with the crest facing up. He took aim and then sent it across the jaguar's throat with a wide swipe. The blade ripped a gaping slash in the jaguar's neck. Blood sprayed and the creature let out a gurgling scream as the fur on its back billowed steam. It fell over on its side and didn't move. Steam rose from the carcass until it shriveled to half its original size.

Rick relaxed and let the helmet fall to his side. Rose went to him, dragging the chain behind her. She knelt and wiped the blood from his face with her sleeve.

"Like I said," Rick sighed, "nothing to worry about."

"I'll be demanding credit for saving your butt in the very near future."

"That? I had that completely under control."

"Uh huh." Rose helped Rick to his feet. She picked up the helmet and handed it to him. "Don't forget your souvenir."

"See why I wanted to bring it with us? Now let's get to the plane before I have to save you from another killer cat."

CHAPTER THIRTY-SEVEN

In the aircraft cabin, Humphrey returned to consciousness disoriented. His vision cleared and Edgar was nowhere to be seen. Humphrey's head pounded like a drum in a marching band. He pulled himself to his feet and went to the doorway. Edgar stood on the closed bow hatch, pulling the slack out of the anchor line.

Being unmoored was the last thing Humphrey needed now. He climbed up atop the cabin. The surface was slick and his shoes slipped. He moved toward Edgar.

"Give it up, boy," he said. "You can't fly this plane."

"It can float downriver for all I care," Edgar said, "as long as I end up away from here."

Edgar had lied to him, slugged him in the jaw, and now he was going to commit the unforgivable offense of using an airplane as a raft. That was the last straw. Humphrey charged Edgar.

Edgar released the anchor line and turned to defend himself. His foot slipped on the deck. He teetered to one side. Shock crossed his face as he windmilled his arms for stability. But gravity would not be denied. He toppled over the side and into the river.

"Dammit," Humphrey said. "Now I have to rescue the louse."

Edgar's head broke the surface. He sputtered and issued a gargled cry for help. Then he slipped underwater again.

Humphrey went to the raft, jumped in, and untied the line. He grabbed the oar and pushed away from the hull.

Edgar surfaced again, this time just barely. Both arms splashed uselessly at the water. Humphrey dug the oar into the water and aimed for Edgar.

Just then, the giant catfish breached beside Edgar, mouth wide open, whiskers straight out at both sides. It came down mouth first over Edgar's head and dove for the river bottom.

Its tail broke the surface and gave Humphrey a wave goodbye as it crashed back into the water.

Humphrey back paddled to stop the raft. The giant catfish could sink him just as easily as it had swallowed Edgar. He waited for his doom.

It did not happen. Perhaps Edgar had been meal enough. Perhaps all the gold and silver in his pockets had caused the fish indigestion. Either explanation was fine with Humphrey.

"Humphrey?" Rick called out.

On the riverbank, Rick had one arm across Rose's shoulder as she held him up. The two looked like they'd been through hell. A makeshift splint on one of his friend's legs was not a good sign. He was also wearing a bloody, antique helmet like a beanie. Rose being shackled to several yards of rusty chain was also cause for some head scratching. Humphrey was just thrilled they were both alive.

Humphrey waved. "You two are a sight for sore eyes. How y'all doing?"

"Ready for a ride home," Rick said.

"That's some fine jewelry you got on your ankle there, Miss Rose," Humphrey said.

"I think it's ostentatious," Rose said. "How about you help me get it off?"

"Y'all sit tight and I'll paddle over."

Humphrey returned to the plane, went into the mechanical room, and found a crowbar and a hammer. He loaded them in the raft and paddled to shore. When he got out of the raft, he observed Rick was splattered with blood.

Rick noticed him staring at it. "No need to worry. It's the blood of a giant jaguar."

"Uh huh," Humphrey said.

Rose eased Rick to the ground and then sat down with her shackled ankle straight out.

Humphrey gave the leg iron a bemused look. "How in hell did you end up in this?"

"A vampire chained me up in a dungeon in a pyramid."

"Well, if you two don't want to talk none about what happened out there, just say so. No need to be insulting."

"We're not kidding," Rick said. "And there's a yellow skunk named Edgar who might show up asking for a ride."

Humphrey wedged the crowbar into the gap between the ends of the bent iron rod that held the shackle closed. Then he began to hit it with a hammer, making sure the blows were directed away from Rose. "Edgar already was here. Tried to steal my damn plane out from under me. He had an unfortunate encounter with a hungry fish."

"I'm not mourning that at all," Rick said.

"The river has dangerous fish?" Rose said.

"Even dangerous to the plane." Humphrey adjusted the crowbar position. "Damn termite fish have been eating at the hull since you left. We need to leave before they sink us. What about Carlos and his men?"

"Spiders, jaguars, vampires, native arrows," Rose said. "It's a long story."

"Well, Edgar lied that the two of you were dead," Humphrey said. "Was kinda hoping he lied about them as well. So, what's with the hat, Rick?"

Rick tapped the helmet with one finger. "Bequeathed by a Spanish conquistador. It's cash in the bank."

Humphrey hit the iron rod again. This time it broke. He pushed it out and released the shackle. Rose began to rub her swollen ankle in relief. Then he and Rose eased Rick into the raft and the three of them made their way back to the plane. The termite fish were still hard at work, and there seemed to be more of them. Rose and Humphrey deposited Rick on the floor of the passenger cabin.

"Losing Carlos does put us in a bind," Humphrey said. "Rick here can't climb up into the cockpit with that leg, no less help fly. I can't manage this plane alone."

"I'll co-pilot," Rose said.

"You?" Humphrey said. "You don't know nothing about flying."

Rose hooked a thumb in Rick's direction. "Neither did he, but you taught him."

"And I'm dumb as a box of rocks compared to Rosie," Rick said. "She can do it."

"I don't know," Humphrey said.

"Are you going to pass up the chance to say you trained the next Amelia Earhart?" Rose said.

"It's her," Rick said, "or we wait here until another pilot floats by."

"Or the termite fish eat the boat," Rose said.

Humphrey bit his lip.

"C'mon, I've seen you do crazier things," Rick said.

"Mostly 'cause you made me," Humphrey said. "All right, Miss Rose. Climb on up and let me show you how to fly a plane."

***

It was hours later when the bump of wheels on tarmac woke Rick up. Night had fallen and all he saw from his poorly angled view out the windows was darkness outside.

He'd managed to fall asleep lying on the cabin floor. His leg didn't hurt much unless he moved it, so he was guessing the fracture was closed, or if he was lucky, hairline. He usually avoided seeing doctors at all costs, but this was one instance when he'd be happy to.

A few minutes after the plane rolled to a stop and the engines shut down, Humphrey entered the cabin.

"Please tell me we're in Cuba," Rick said.

"Yep." Humphrey ran his fingers through his hair. "Now we gotta make for my plane pretty quick while the airport is closed. We don't want to be here when people start asking what happened to Carlos and his crew. The vampires and jaguars story ain't gonna go over well."

"I guess Rose did okay up there?"

"You know, I have to say she did. And you were right, she's loads smarter than you."

"Uh, thanks?"

"I'll go pre-flight my plane," Humphrey said, "then we'll get you over there."

Humphrey disappeared into the darkness. Moments later, Rose entered the cabin. The open cockpit's wind had blown her red hair almost straight back and she was trying to claw it down into a normal position. Dirt stained her cheeks beneath where the goggles had protected her eyes and it made her look like she wore a white mask.

"I love your new look," Rick said.

"Someone who needs help getting out of this plane shouldn't antagonize the person who will be helping him."

"Looks like you co-piloted us here okay."

"I was mostly throwing switches and reading maps and turning dials. But between the two of us we made it to Cuba." She paused. "Humphrey is actually a good and conscientious pilot."

"I've said that for years. Don't tell me this experience has bred some mutual respect between the two of you?"

"Don't be ridiculous."

Humphrey stuck his head back in the door. "My plane's ready when you are."

"Then let's go home," Rick said.

CHAPTER THIRTY-EIGHT

Two weeks later
As far as Rick was concerned, being stuck in the Treasure Hunters Antiques shop was one step short of a prison sentence.

The doctor he'd seen when they returned to Savannah had done a fine job setting his leg. He'd been lucky that it had been a hairline fracture. But the plaster cast and crutches meant he wasn't driving, in fact not even walking far from the shop. Rose had been great about carrying the full load while he was healing, but he hated feeling trapped.

Worse, he hated feeling useless. Right now, Rose was out picking up an estate they'd purchased, and they'd had to hire some help to load and unload the stuff from the truck. That wasn't financially sustainable given that the sale of the helmet barely covered the cost of the Mexico trip, and it didn't do anything for his ego to watch someone do the work he was supposed to do. And the work he was doing instead minding the store could have been done by a shop girl.

Standing behind the counter would have been murder on his leg, so he'd taken one of the rocking chairs for sale, moved it beside the register, and set an ottoman in front of it. Settled into this seat, he could see anyone entering the shop and into most of the aisles of goods, though the far corner was out of his line of sight.

The bell rang and announced the opening of the front door. In stepped Matty Mahoney. Rick sighed and stood up.

Rose had a dislike-on-sight predisposition for most of Rick's friends, and Matty was one of the reasons. Some of Rick's business actions balanced on the line between honest and dishonest. Matty's usually crashed through the line without braking. The weasel-looking little man wore a tattered fedora and a workingman's shirt and trousers, which was ironic since Rick was sure the man hadn't worked a straight job since his teenage paper route. He carried a stained, brown paper bag in one hand.

Matty cast furtive glances up and down the street through the front window. He had the look of a man holding a pair of threes with his life savings already thrown in the pot. Apparently satisfied that he'd entered the shop unobserved, he turned to see Rick. Matty assumed an unconvincing smile.

"Ricky, old pal," he said. "How's tricks?"

"Not bad. Long time, no see, Matty."

"Well, you know me. Always a new deal, always on the move."

"Always a step ahead of the police," Rick said.

"Oh, he he. Such a kidder, Ricky, really. But I've got something for you, something one of your high roller customers would like."

Matty put the paper bag on the counter. He reached in and pulled out a life-sized stone-sculpted human hand. Rick raised an eyebrow. The stone looked like jade.

"May I?" Rick said.

"Sure, sure. That's solid jade there, a hundred percent."

Rick picked up the hand. The heft and the coldness confirmed it was solid stone. He turned the piece under the light. The polished surface was perfectly smooth and the seams between stones nearly imperceptible. This piece was the real deal.

"What's a nice girl like you," Rick said to the jade hand, "doing with a mug like this guy?"

"Hey, watch it, Ricky. This is on the up-and-up, totally legit. I knew a guy who knew a guy and I got it cheap. Rich folks are getting desperate in this Depression, you know?"

Rick knew they were. He'd seen them come in to the shop ready to dump serious heirlooms to make ends meet. "You can leave it here on consignment. I'll pay you when it sells."

Matty's face fell. "Oh, Ricky, that ain't no good. I'm looking for cash now. I got some pressing bills, you know?"

Given Matty's history, Rick guessed Matty's bill collectors were the kind who charged high interest and broke bones for non-payment.

"What do you say you buy it, huh?" Matty said.

"What do you want for it?"

Matty gave him a price. It was more money than Rick and Rose had in their savings account. But it was also a third of what this piece was worth, even just for the weight of the jade.

"This thing isn't cursed, is it?" Rick said with a smile.

Fear filled Matty's face. "What? No! Nothing like that. C'mon, Ricky. What do you say? Help a fellow out in a jam?"

Rick rubbed a finger against the hand's glossy finish. This was exactly the kind of piece he was always telling Rose they should buy, something good for a high-end sale with a low-end acquisition price. Things might get financially tight for a while, but when this sold, they'd be on Easy Street for sure.

"You have a deal," Rick said.

Matty looked so relieved, Rick was afraid the guy was going to hug and kiss him. "That's my boy. I tell everyone, Rick's the one who'll give you a fair shake. Trust me, you won't regret this."

Rick had been holding the hand for a few moments. It still felt unnaturally cold. Second thoughts about this purchase popped into his head. He pushed them away. He needed to trust his gut on this one. Matty was right. He wouldn't regret it.

Once he'd explained it to Rose, that is.

AFTERWORD

Rick and Rose have made it home again, but it was a close one. If you haven't enjoyed their first two adventures you can pick up *Quest for the Queen's Temple* and *Voyage to Blackbeard's Island* and share some of their other close calls.

In these stories I try to weave as much actual history and actual science into the fantastic as possible. I think it makes the story more credible and sometimes the restrictions that reality puts in place force me to be more creative, and I love that challenge. Let's see what kind of facts back up this fiction.

Rick and Rose are in search of a lost city from the Aztec Empire. For two hundred years starting about 1325, the Aztecs built and maintained an empire of city-states in what is now Mexico, possibly as many as five hundred cities at its peak. A combination of military force and diplomatic alliances bonded these cities together. However, Rick's Lost City of Gold, Tezpaluca, was not one of them. I made that place up.

Aztec culture delivered many technological innovations in construction and agriculture. The description of Tezpaluca is an amalgam of a number of actual Aztec city ruins. They kept a very accurate 365-day calendar. The weapons the villagers use in the story are all accurate representations of Aztec weapons, especially the atlatl used by Ocotlan and others.

The S-shaped atlatl had a hook and a groove in the wood at one end where projectiles were placed. It could launch solid objects as well as fearsome multi-barbed darts tipped with fish bone, copper, flint, or obsidian points. The conquistadors said that the sharp darts of the atlatl could pierce armor. The atlatl had an extreme reach of two hundred and forty-three feet with devastating accuracy at lesser ranges.

Aztecs served a multitude of deities, including Huitzilopochtli (god of war and of the sun) and Quetzalcoatl ("Feathered Serpent"), and Tlaloc, the rain god. Tezcatlipoca was their god of the night, but the rituals I've associated with his worship in this book are fictional. However, it is true that as part of some religious rites, Aztecs practiced both bloodletting (offering one's own blood) and human sacrifice as part of their religious practices. Those practices were what sent me down the vampire myth rabbit hole for Itztli and the rulers of Tezpaluca, but as far as I know there was no vampire-equivalent in Aztec mythology.

Spanish conquistadors arrived in the early 1500s in search of gold and other riches. Once they found them, the Aztecs were doomed. Their vast military was no match for a smaller group of Spaniards with 16th century technology. In addition, European diseases took an awful toll on a population with no natural immunity. With the help of a turncoat city-state, the Spaniards sacked the Aztec capital in what is now Mexico City, and the empire began its collapse.

Would it be possible for there to be a lost city waiting to be discovered in 1938? Many cities were swallowed by the jungle after the empire's collapse. One Maya city, similar to Aztec civilization, Calakmul was discovered by Cyrus Lundell in 1931 deep into the jungle of Mexico. It may have had a population of 50,000 people living among 6,750 structures. So certainly Rick and Rose could have found one. Now with modern LIDAR technology, new potential cities are being rediscovered, and new details about current sites are coming to light.

On their trek to the city, Rick and Rose eat a guanabana. Also called a soursop, the fruit is pear-shaped with a dark green skin covered with big thorns. On the inside is a white, soft, creamy flesh. I'm told it smells a little like pineapple, but it tastes more like a combination of strawberries, citrus and bananas. I hope to try one someday. (That's not an invitation for people to start overnighting me guanabanas!)

There was certainly no shortage of deadly creatures in Central American jungles to draw antagonist inspiration from. The first I selected was the jaguar.

Jaguars are the only big cat in the Americas and the third largest in the world. They look a lot like African leopards, but have more complex spots, often with a dot in the center. Representations of the jaguar show up in the art and archaeology of cultures in Central and South America. They are excellent hunters and, unlike most big cats, excellent swimmers. They will even eat a caiman! Jaguars live alone, and are territorial, which made them a perfect fit for the vampire's needs in the story.

On the road to the village, our heroes are beset by giant black widow spiders. In real life, the species is widespread and you might have one in your own back yard, though on a much smaller scale. A large female black widow spider can only grow to about 1.5 inches including the leg span. Males are half the size of the female or even smaller. The spider has potent venom, fifteen times more potent than that of rattlesnakes. But luckily, there isn't much of it in a tiny spider. However, a bite can cause muscle and chest pain. The pain also may spread to the abdomen, producing cramping and nausea. If you are really having a bad day, you may also get restlessness, anxiety, breathing difficulty, sweating, and swelling in the hands and feet, but rarely at the bite site. So, stay away from these little monsters.

I wish I could tell you that the termite fish that attack the plane's hull were real, but they are not. Termites really bore through wood, and there are multiple sea creatures that do the same, but nothing like the termite fish. There are giant catfish just like the one that finished off Edgar, though.

The Aeromarine 75 was a real plane used in the early 1900s for mail and passenger service. An internet search will get you a ton of cool vintage pictures of it. I love how the passengers got an enclosed cabin, but the pilots had to deal with the elements from an open cockpit.

This book could not have been possible without the help of my wonderful beta readers Donna Fitzpatrick and Deb DeAlteriis. Also, a big thanks goes out to all the people at Severed Press whose editing and artwork make my Saturday matinee monster stories look so good.

And lastly, thanks to all you readers who give my books a shot in paper, digital, and audiobook forms. I couldn't invest the time to do this without the payoff of knowing you enjoyed it. Keep on reading!

I don't know about you but I've got a bad feeling about the jade hand Matty just sold to Rick. I'm betting it sends Rick and Rose out on another adventure. What kind of adventure? I have no idea yet. Once I do, I'll be sharing it with all of you.

-Russell James

www.ingramcontent.com/pod-product-compliance
Lightning Source LLC
Chambersburg PA
CBHW061232170626
46809CB00007B/2642